THE WADE SCANDAL

• • • • • • • • • • • • • •

MICHAEL DE'SHAZER II

4/27/06

Published by The Wensor Company, LLC
Memphis, Tennessee

Printed in the United States of America.

Three may keep a secret, if two of them are dead.

—R. Saunders, 1735

PART I

THE END

She knew what she had to do...

His journal fell from her hands to the floor. Her shaking hands gripped her heated face as tears poured through the cracks between her fingers. She had never cried so much in her life. She was losing her breath as air lunged in and out of her at an abnormally fast rate. She let out a high-pitched scream as she fell sideways from her husband's favorite chair onto the floor. Again, she screamed. The sound-proof walls prevented anyone from hearing her cry. Lying there, she painfully suffered in her own anguish. She felt the pain in her chest as she endured the heartache from the overwhelming revelations revealed from the pages of her late husband's journal.

"Lies!" she cried. "All lies!" Chills ran rapidly up and down her back and spread throughout her body. She banged the wooden floor with her right fist. Tear drops hit the floor as she banged harder and harder until her arm finally gave out and her entire body collapsed. Face down on the floor, she moaned agonizingly, *"Why!?"*

as her voice broke and nothing but wheezes escaped from her mouth. Her head became hotter, and her cheeks became tense. She rolled over slowly onto her back as more tears rolled down her face without direction; she felt some run into her ears; she tasted others as they ran into her mouth. The questions of *why* haunted her in her heated, impassioned mourning. She desperately tried to answer the questions that bombarded her mind all at once. *Did he truly love me? Why would he lie to me? What else had he lied about? Why me?*

She let out an intense, deafening scream that temporarily impaired her own ears. But what did her ears matter? *What mattered?* Screaming more, she picked up the journal that had fallen with her and threw it with a vengeance at the mirror that stood across the room. It bounced off the mirror, falling once again to the floor. Quickly, she rose and ran towards the mirror. Upon seeing her reflection, she struck the mirror with her fist, penetrating it with her wedding ring, causing the mirror to shatter. Pieces of the mirror darted onto the floor and some into her flesh. But what did either of these matter, floor or flesh? She fell onto the glass, painfully absorbing the sharp incisions as her blood stained some of the scattered pieces. She looked down at one of the bigger pieces of mirror. It was sharp and fairly resembled a dagger. She let out another cry as she looked into her eyes through the dagger-shaped piece.

Sitting up, she grasped the dagger with both hands and raised it from the floor up towards her face. She extended her arms so that they were straight, the point of the dagger pointing towards the floor. She gripped it tightly, released the sharp piece of mirror with her blood-drenched right hand to wipe the tears from her eyes, and regained her grasp even tighter. With great force, she impelled it into her stomach. She gasped for breath and fell to the floor. Before she could die from her own self-affliction, her heartache killed her first. Her eyes closed as she lay dead, her husband's journal laying next to her.

* * *

This is the story of the president, his wife, and the events that history would not mention.

PART II

THE BEGINNING

CHAPTER I

Surrounded by a syndicate of "political idiots" (for lack of a better term), the president was playing the Security Council like a fiddle. Everything was going according to his plans. Seated around the Council Room of the White House were the Secretary of State, Secretary of Treasury, Secretary of Defense, the Central Intelligence Advisor, Chief of Staff, and Counsel to the President. The Council meeting had been in session for an hour now.

"What happened to the rest of the letter?" asked the Secretary of Defense.

"We don't know. All that we know is that it was from one of our ambassadors in Iraq, Alan Dell, who caught a sudden case of suffocation in a plastic bag three hours ago," replied Robert Parnell, Central Intelligence Advisor.

"So that's it? That's all we got? We have a letter from a dead ambassador vaguely describing secret measures to mechanically alter humans in Iraq. Are we doing some kind of rendition of X-Men? What else do we have?" asked the president.

"Nothing, as of now," answered Parnell.

Meet Robert Parnell: the biggest patsy since Lee Harvey Oswald. He was following his script exactly the way he was supposed to, except he didn't know it, like the rest of the Council members (minus the president). Intelligence Advisor Parnell was an older man, a Vietnam vet with gray hair, a sharp and well maintained British accent, and a once brilliant mind that was slowly disintegrating. He was respected because of his elderly age but not revered.

The president shifted in his chair. "Well, as of now, are we doing anything to retrieve information?"

"Actually, that is nearly impossible at this time, as we have no major intelligence contacts in the Iraqi underground. They've worked hard to insure that we didn't have easy access. They hate us, Mr. President. You know that."

The president stared at the floor for a few moments, taking his sweet time. "Look, I have a three o'clock on the golf course this afternoon. Read the letter from Mr. Dell one more time."

Parnell read the letter once again.

Dear Sir,

It has come to my attention that there has arisen a new threat to our national security. It is to my knowledge that humanity as we know it has been evolving into a new creation. This new creation is being biologically engineered by captured neurologists, aerodynamic engineers, and researchers of various fields of science from the Middle East, northern Africa, and India.

These captured researchers and engineers are believed to have been rearranging the nervous system of human experiments.

It is also believed that these captured scientists have been forced to develop methods to implant aero-mechanisms and other devices inside their human subjects. These inhumane experiments have been code-named "The Baghdad Project." According to my intelligence, these human experiments are being produced with the intention to create a new race of humans with unnatural abilities to be used by radical Middle Eastern extremist regimes.

These experiments have broken many international regulations. These regulation offenses include the acts of illegally abducting citizens from their country of origin and manipulating human DNA. It is speculated that these human experiments would have the ability to exert immense amounts of devastating energy and plunge hundreds of feet in the air without any mechanical aid whatsoever.

Taking, what I believe to be, necessary precaution in light of this information, I hereby urge that the United States take action to end these practices and learn of the methods used by the Iraqi government and terrorist organizations. It is also

"The end."

The president tapped his finger on his lip and then pointed at Parnell. "See what you can get. Oh, and cover the cause of death on our Iraqi ambassador. Also, talk to some of our other officials in Iraq and keep them quiet. Somebody, call Effie in here." The Counsel to the President immediately knocked on the entrance door twice, summoning the admin directly outside the Council Room. Instantaneously, the admin appeared standing inside the open door.

"Effie, see if my caddy's ready and get me a bottled water."

She dutifully nodded and exited, closing the door. The president stood as all the Council members stood simultaneously. "I'll see you all in six hours. Get me some facts, ladies and gentlemen. He raised his arm, palm up, inviting the Security Council out of the Council room.

* * *

Six hours later at precisely 8:30 p.m., all of the National Security Council was seated in the Council Room awaiting the president. He always made it a point to be five minutes late—it was an authority measure.

"Ladies and Gentlemen...oh, and you, Parnell," started the president. Everyone chuckled, everyone including the president who always found marvelous humor in his self-perceived comical remarks. Even Parnell laughed, hoping to himself privately that the president would croak at that very moment. The president's smile wore off and the smiles of the Council also faded in perfect unison. "What do you all have for me? Facts this time, I'm hoping."

State Secretary Carla Santiago stood. Ms. Santiago was a slightly heavyset woman; however, it was noticeable that once in her lifetime she could have been quite the knockout. She was the extremely punctual, overly orderly type.

"Yes, Mr. President. Some of our people talked with the other US officials in Iraq. We have discovered that none of them were privy to the information forwarded to us by Mr. Dell. Furthermore, they have expressed the high implausibility of the existence of the bio-engineering human 'Baghdad Project' that was detailed in the Ambassador Dell letter."

"Good. I'll sleep better tonight. Do we have any other information?"

Others made remarks, reiterating what Santiago previously stated. The case was closed. Then, Parnell stood. "Mr. President, even though we think this may have been some sick prank by the Iraqis after the horrible homicide of Dell, we can't just sit on this."

The president looked up at the ceiling as if considering what Parnell was saying. "You're right. We need to find out why Dell was killed. Remember, keep this investigation under wraps. Start a file and make sure it remains classified. I don't want any press, at least for the next few days. Do what you guys do and get it done. This information was never presented to me. Dismissed."

Parnell stood again, this time almost jumping to his feet. "What about the Baghdad Project?"

The president looked at Parnell and then at the rest of the Council, smiling, and said, "There is no Baghdad Project." He had a serious face again. "Dismissed— Parnell, you stay." The members of the Security Council rose and departed, all except Parnell.

The president looked at Parnell as the door eased to a close. "Resign," said the president simply and in utter casualness as if not comprehending the weight of his very rehearsed statement. Parnell was finally getting it: the pink slip, the boot, the kick to the curb—he was being let go. He looked entirely stumped as if the president had told him to, well, resign or something.

And then, there it was. Parnell squeaked out a predictable, "*What?*"

"Yes, Parnell, I believe it is time that you resign from your position here and move on. I can see you're not happy here. You're definitely not happy or you are simply insane."

The president paused as if he was giving his inaugural address, pacing his spill. Parnell saw this as the perfect point to chime in once again, "What are you saying?"

"You came in here today presenting a letter that your intelligence picked up about chemically engineered, dying Iraqis with no proof, no evidence. And worse, you did it in front of my very impressionable, new Security Council without advising me prior to your ludicrous presentation."

"This letter isn't ludicrous!"

The president stood up from his chair, remembering his afternoon golf course-rehearsed lines regarding the release of Mr. Parnell. The president already knew about the information contained in the letter. What Parnell didn't know was that the president was involved in the Baghdad Project scheme himself. Parnell was George the Curious Little Monkey in this one and needed to be pinched. Nope, there were no more bananas for this guy Parnell. "You disregarded protocol. It's simple. Resign, retire, I don't care," said the president offhandedly yet stern.

"What do you expect me to do?" asked Parnell. The president thought to himself immediately: *Is this what a head intelligence advisor asks when he's being let go—"What do you expect me to do?"* For someone advising in the field of intelligence, he was not displaying his field of expertise. Old age was beating down Parnell's mental consistency. Off remarks like this was not unusual.

"I don't care. Go home and tell your wife that your department was down-sized." The president shed a half-smile at his self-humoring witticism. "I'll tell you what to tell your wife. Really. I'll even tell you how to tell the people across America who really don't care anyway. Tomorrow, you will announce your resignation and retirement at a special press conference right here in the White House." The president had planned this out for the last six months. It just so happened to be the day before the old man's seventy-fifth birthday. Retirement age birthdays were always good for announcing retirement: there were always fewer questions asked in the media curiosity department. At this wonderful point, the inquiries of *"why"* weren't the foremost asked questions, but the cheers of celebration and inquiries of *"what will you do next?"* rank highly. Plus, the old man was ten years overdue anyway. At this quarter in the game, the only one who would actually care about his retirement would obviously be Parnell's wife. That was exactly the way the president wanted it. No one wondering too much—less press sniffing for dirt on an all-of-a-sudden retirement. He was going to ensure that everyone knew this was Parnell's own decision in interest of himself and country.

Parnell was overcome with disbelief. The president could not just give him the boot like that, he thought. On second thought, yes, he could—third, fourth, and fifth thought the same, as well. Parnell had had a good run; only to be shot down swiftly with a forced retirement. *Why was the president requesting his resignation on this small procedural incident?* That action was not enough for losing one's job. Plus, a discovery of this magnitude was commonly handled the same way with prompt briefing, even if it was in a Council meeting. It was current, and it was urgent news. There must have been more to the story. The president saw the old man's mind working.

"Look, I'm going to ask you to face the music like a man," said the president as he was taken back by his own statement to his childhood years of peer-pressuring using the take-it-like-a-man tactic. He had always been good at swaying people to do things in his favor (like voting for him). Now was one of those times when it would come in handy again. "Don't be difficult in this. It'll be very simple. You'll tell a cheap joke; talk about the things you have accomplished; speak of the hard times; captivate people with stories of how you persevered through those times; give details of what you came to learn; and metaphorically explain why it is now time for you to retire—just like that, in relatively the same order. You can do it. I believe in you."

Parnell's disintegrating mind randomly induced him to be blunt with the president. It appeared as though Parnell was thrown into a farther world of shock that seemingly put a backbone in him. "With all due respect, Mr. President, I have served as the Central Intelligence Advisor for the last twenty years. To be here and listen to you boldly tell me to give up the position that I earned through my desire to protect and serve this country with the utmost hard work and dedication...this disgusts me. Your lack of respect for that throughout your term and your incompetence in your own position causes me to question any of your decisions and especially your decision to request my resignation. I would like to in turn make a request for you. I would suggest that you reconsider your insipid demand. I have stood aside for the past six months of your presidency, watching you do some odd deeds that could very well put you in the position in which you have just placed me. Mark my words, Gordon. Your time will come soon if you continue in your attempt to force my retirement."

Parnell changed moods in an instant from boldness to insouciance quicker than the drop of a dime. Then, he paused again. "Mr. President, if that is your desire, however, I will..." he paused for a moment. He looked the president square in the eyes and continued. "However, I will consider your request and we can discuss this matter at a later time."

Negotiation class 101: a quick resolution is to halfway agree to a point and suggest resolve until later negotiations. The president knew this tactic. It was not going to work.

"No," the president said. "I have decided already for you. Let's take the easy way on this one. The easy way would definitely be easier for the both of us, especially you." A small threat, but it was, in no way, idle. The conversation went back and forth for awhile. If this were a ball game the score would be: President- 198, Parnell-negative something. Probably the only thing consistent about Parnell was his tendency to be inconsistent and make statements that were way out in left field. And thus, nearing the end of the conversation, Parnell's path in life, or rather to the grave, was set. He would give his retirement speech tomorrow at a special press conference just for the old patriot. Parnell was walking defeated out of the door, when he switched once again. The president established that this couldn't be healthy as Parnell had another mental lapse and was now conservatively begging for his job. The president decided it was time to bring out the big guns and seal the deal. "Parnell, I know. I know about the Baricon and the money. I know about your deal. I'm going to try to save you some embarrassment. You've made a huge mistake, and that's an understatement. You've committed one of the worst crimes against this country since Benedict Arnold. Your secret engagements are probably worse. You could be your own adjective and preponderate in meaning the very word 'treachery.' The funny thing is that you thought I would never find out. You thought that this was going to happen without anybody saying such a word as 'hey.' You are lucky it's not you out there lying somewhere with your head plastic-bagged. I'm giving you an opportunity; it would be in your best interest to take it."

At noon the next day, Parnell gave his retirement speech.

* * *

In the Press Room in the White House, Parnell was standing before about twenty cameras ready to give his speech. "Today," Parnell began, "I will spare the political heavy-handed words, which are so famous in this room, in light of this great day. I would like to make a note: Right now, my job is to speak, and your job as the audience is to listen—if you finish before I do, please let me know.

"In every individual's life, there comes those rare moments when it becomes apparent that it's time to put on your blinkers in the car of life and make a decision at, what I call, a big Y-junction. You are presented with two choices: either you can go left, or you can go right. Sometimes, you can be in that right lane, getting ready to coast along in the right direction, because that's where you think you want to go. Then, all of a sudden, something amazing happens...you see the sign.

"Well, I'm at that junction. Today is my seventy-fifth birthday and I'm at another big Y-junction once again. Last week, I was planning on coasting along the highway of life when I saw that sign. After doing the same duty year after year, I was making the same turn in life. And everyone knows once you take a considerable amount of turns the same way, you're driving in circles."

Parnell's mind was taking a turn of its own now, right into memory lane as he paused. Then, he remembered where he was and was back on track after and an awkward fifteen seconds. "Once you do the same thing over and over again, you get to a certain point when you realize that maybe what you are doing is not serving as productivity as it once did. Moreover, I believe I've reached that point in my life. I've reached that point where I am changing lanes and moving into another phase of my life. I am reaching that phase where I am beginning to realize that driving in circles will no longer benefit those in which my duty should benefit.

"Moving along, I'd like to share something with all of you today. One thing I've learned in my field through the years is that national security is the second most important thing to people. People will sacrifice their personal desires and ambitions, even morals, for safety. Some people's safety is religion. Some people's safety is a job. Some people's safety is a spouse. It is human nature to want safety. I've worked for decades to insure the safety of this country. Almost nothing is held more dearly to me than my assurance of this nation's security—nothing except *my* safety of course."

Parnell smiled; the press didn't. His cheap joke didn't receive as much as a slight grin. The press wasn't concerned.

"However, like I said, security is only the second most important thing to us. The question is then asked: What is it? What do we, as humans, desire the most? I can attest to you it is not love, if some of you were getting that popularly accepted apprehension. No, indeed it is truly hope. Hope is what love is based on. Hope gives you a reason to seek security. Hope is important in the lives of all of us. Hope is the backbone of this country, along with taxes of course. It is this hope that has brought men to fight for rights against tyranny, persecution, and oppression. It is hope that brought women to fight for the right to vote. It was hope that brought about the signing of the Emancipation Proclamation. It was hope that brought about the declaration which stated that this nation was independent and free. It was hope that brings us all out of our shells and into the world to thrive. Furthermore, thriving is what we live for in this life.

"So, in my life in which I have chosen to thrive, I have decided that it is now time that I move onto a new realm for the very reason we live. Hope allows me to believe that there is something better out there, and my passion to thrive and serve my nation brings me to leave my duty up to a fresh, younger thinker who can pick up where I left off and protect a great nation as we head into a brighter future. This is my left turn, and today I'm on a different road. I hereby announce my resignation from my office as Central Intelligence Advisor to the President. Well, I'm not sure what to say from here other than Godspeed." He really didn't know what to say and it was very random, but what else could one expect from the old man.

As the now former Central Intelligence Advisor exited the podium, while shaking hands with the president (kind of like they were real buddies), there arose the inevitable press ruckus. The ruckus was normal: everyone had a question, and if a reporter in the press room didn't have one, then that individual was simply not a reporter. Every single solitary soul in the White House press room had at least one inquiry.

The president was right concerning no one caring about Parnell's retirement, if one was to look at the event from retrospect. Many questions here and over there came up, yet none of them were concerning any of Parnell's other reasons for retiring, but rather who would fill the empty space of the former intelligence advisor. Parnell really didn't know, but he said that the Security Council was presently considering the to-be-appointed intelligence advisor. The president already had that part handled—he knew just the man for the job.

CHAPTER II

After a vicious campaign season, Gordon Wade had swept the presidential elections with seventy percent of the American vote, exemplifying the word "landslide." It was the first all-out take of the elections in a long time. The even more staggering detail about the wipeout election was that Gordon was a member of the (until his advent) practically non-influential Independent political party.

The president was a smart fellow, always thinking ahead of the game; and if there was one thing the president knew, it was that politics was a game. His philosophy was that politics was not similar to, kind-of-like, or of resemblance to a game: it was a synonym for the word "game." The players were the businesses, lobbyists, politicians, and those other people...the public. The public filled out ballots to elect the politicians and wrote out checks to economically elect businesses into the mainstream of the game. Lobbyists kind of drifted in the middle somewhere. It was a dangerous game and only the best (usually liars) survived. It was not always what a person knew or even whom, but how much money a person had and how well they could manipulate. In politics, everyone was working an angle. Manipulation was the key, so the most important part to remember about politics was nothing was what it seemed. Nothing ought to have been judged merely on face value.

He was a middle-age man, married, no kids, with a dog. Gordon never really saw his dog, but he could recall that the dog's name was Spot, or maybe it was Spike. To Gordon, it was more of a trivia question than a pet.

He went to Columbia University, obtained his undergraduate, and went back to his alma mater for law school the following year. Columbia Law School was a good prestigious name that went well on his qualification's resume when he went out for the New York State House of Representatives. It was a lowly position in the immense, ever-expanding political world, but it was a step closer to his ultimate objective. Later, he went out for the US House to get closer to that objective but was beaten by the other guy. He practiced law for years as a litigator, pinching pennies, saving for his next campaign for the US House. After his second go-around, he was successful in becoming a US Representative in the House. After serving a term, he set his sights on the US Senate and won by a slim, hundred-vote margin. His major platform when he went out for the US Senate was domestic terrorism prevention. His terrorism platform was ironic because he was a quiet and secret member of the Baricon, a major Middle Eastern "terrorist organization" (or so they called it) on the United States' international threat file.

The Baricon depended on Gordon's ascendance up the political ladder. They could have given him the financial support he needed easily when he was in the Senate or the House, but a monetary transaction would have been an insipid move at that stage—too much of an eyebrow raiser. They had to let him fly on his own all the way to the top, to the position of President of the United States. Then, it would be time to exchange supports; it was all disingenuously plotted out. If his wife knew, she'd kill him. All would eventually be revealed about his secret affiliations with the Baricon, and it would take a while to explain. The time would come (he hoped). There were many secrets, very many secrets.

Her name was Pamela Nicole Wade. He met her first semester of law school on a cool, autumn day in one of the amphitheaters on campus. She was looking for the women's dorms—she knew where they were. He offered to help her find her way; in fact, he suggested that he assist her search for the dormitories because the campus could be so tricky to get around—it wasn't. She had just broken up with her boyfriend two weeks prior to their acquaintance; subsequently, this thing led to that, that thing led to this, and so on. The thing about romance is that it is amorously doomed to repeat itself.

The day of graduation, he proposed; she said yes. They got married and lived happily ever after—how quickly the Titanic would hit the iceberg. If she truly loved him, however, which she really did, the great ship would hold sail, hopefully. On the other hand, lies and deceit have a common tendency of severing marriages. Gordon knew their marriage was strong; with luck, it would be strong enough. He figured that if he could run the greatest superpower in the world, then he could easily manage any domestic affair with his wife. This was with luck, of course. Given the fact he loved her so much, if she was to leave, he would not contest her departure. He implanted this notion deep within his mind; unfortunately, he didn't believe it, nor could he halfway fool himself. On the bright side, for now, they were in love—how quickly the meteor would hit.

She was tall, about 5'9, with flowing, dark hair. Middle-aged like her spouse, yet her smooth skin was absolutely flawless. To Gordon, she was the epitome of comeliness. He once complemented that, on a bad day, her beauty would top any Aphrodite or Helen of Troy. She was the expensive-type gal. She wore Prada and Louis Vuiton, but her expensive taste was not a thing of vanity but mere desire for nice, name-brand vanity possessions.

They were in love—how quickly the great Roman Empire would crumple. When the famous general Julius Caesar crossed the Rubicon River to face the immeasurable forces of the great Pompeii in battle, he bravely claimed the famed words *"Alia iacta est!"*—the die is cast! The president was living a secret life all this time, and every moment was a gamble. He approached their bedroom door, slowly exhaling, saying under his breath the same words as he did so many times passed, *"Alia iacta est."*

She was the decorator, so the bedroom was nothing short of captivating. It was not simple, yet it was not overly ostentatious. Feng Shui would be the term. The curtains were burgundy, the feel was mahogany, and the mood was mellow with light vibrancy. The gigantic king-sized bed provided a colossal presence in the room. The room was vast in space. Basically, it was swanky in all detail. She loved it, and he loved that she loved it. He could have lived with the bare essentials of a pallet, pillow, and restroom. Also, Pamela ensured even the master bath was posh in the word's truest sense. The shower was basically a waterfall with water trickling down the encircling walls. She had it designed like that in remembrance of their honeymoon cruise to Cozemel, Mexico, nearly twenty years ago.

When Gordon walked in, his wife was watching the inside of her eyelids. The glow from the 70" flat screen was shimmering over her face as the TV watched her. She was not asleep though—it was too early. She was merely "resting the eyes" as she did most late evenings after a long day of press, benefits, speeches, and so forth. Being the First Lady was not a duty to sleep on. Likewise, she was not sleeping at this time of evening, just "resting the eyes."

"Honey, I'm home!" he said after he closed the door, as he walked behind the recliner, touching her shoulder. She had a book resting in her arms. She was watching television and reading at the same time again. His wife could never do a single thing at once, except rest her eyes. Her eyes still closed, a smile formed across her face. She pivoted the back of her head upward so that her face could ascend to receive a kiss from her dearly loved husband. He held her chin gently as he gave her a peck of affection.

Her eyes opened, and she asked with a beaming and loving tinge, "How was your day, dear?"

"Quite interesting," Gordon said.

"How was Parnell's retirement speech? I missed it. I was at a middle school earlier talking to some young people about being leaders of the future, kind of like my husband," Pamela said, still smiling. That was another distinguishing characteristic about the First Lady. She seemed to always have a smile on her face.

"It was quite interesting like I said. He used some kind of analogy about a Y-junction and turns in life. I'm glad he's finally retired, though. It was definitely the old man's time to go."

"Oh yeah, honey? You never liked that poor old man in the first place, did you?" She said this yawning, rousing from her resting of the eyes.

"Now, why would you say that? I never had anything against Parnell. If anything, I revered the man. He is a great hero for his amazing efforts in Vietnam and his great agency service up until recently. His British accent has been floating in the White House longer than any of the rest of the 'old chaps' as he would say. It was his time, and he just didn't realize it, that's all. I heard that during the last presidency, they tried to get him to retire but he just couldn't hear the fat lady singing and decided that it wasn't his time to leave yet. It was time someone put a little brass to his—"

"Dear! See? That's what I'm talking about, right there. Now, come on. What was it? Was it his gray hair? It was his cute little British accent, wasn't it? Women like British accents, you know. Ah, dear, were you feeling threatened that the poor old man was going to take your honey with his sexy British twang?"

The president came to the epiphany that jovial affection at this moment would be the perfect deflection from the talk about Parnell's retirement and a window of opportunity into other, more romantic affairs. He noticed that she wasn't seeing that same window of opportunity. He hopped over in front of the recliner, letting her legs down and lifting her into his arms. Attempting with his feeble might, he spoke with maybe one of the worst imitated British accents saying, "Well, the bloody chap was getting in the way, and now he's gone, so no need for worrying. I'm the only lad; in fact, I'm the king lad! Now it's time for me to elope with my queen. He smothered his smiling face into hers, rubbing his nose against hers in a teasingly vehement manner.

Holding his face with both hands, she started gasping for the oxygen outside his facial blockade. She smiled beamingly, yelling, "Stop you bloody Brit! English isn't my type! And wait until I tell my husband. You know he's the president back in the States. You're in bwig twouble, mister!"

He smiled; carrying her now, her legs wrapped around him. He then gently placed her onto the bed. "Well, your husband does not have to know. We can keep this business between us, aye?"

"You're not British! I could tell first from your fake accent that faded from Middle Eastern to Jamaican, and now its all American. Gosh, stick to your role!"

The president hesitated briefly, then maintained his character as the sweeping, full-of-beans romantic and said, "Come here, beautiful."

She declined, to his surprise. She began her prying, saying, "Wait, wait, dear, tell me more about the advisor's retirement." He rolled his eyes like a six year-old being reprimanded, blowing air into her face showing regret for the loss of the (otherwise) moment of verbal nothingness. She really wanted to talk about this Parnell and retirement thing. Gordon thought to himself quickly: *Got to get off subject, got to reach ultimate goal, got to defer this woman from current event interest.* This would be no easy task. He figured that maybe if he rambled for awhile not really addressing what she was inquiring, she would lose interest. And maybe he would throw in a shocker at the end, if it was necessary.

Rambling was a major lesson learned in the acclaimed school of political rhetoric. Public speaking on things he knew nothing about, which happened more often than on occasion, required precise verbal circumlocution. It was called over-the-head addressing. He was good at this art of circumlocution. He analogized, emotionalized, and then hit the ball out of the park with the kicker. He was good. (At deception, that is).

He started, "National security is like a tricycle. A tricycle needs three wheels to stand up, right? Well, imagine that the three wheels of the National Security Council tricycle are the military advisors, intelligence advisors, and the financial advisors. All three of these advising areas hold up the tricycle that is the Security Council. If one of those wheels is getting old and beginning to flatten, it is our duty to, if you will, change that wheel. Parnell's retirement was like a change of wheels. He was getting old and his productivity was slacking. It was time to get rid of the slack and find a new wheel." He rambled more about national security this, national security that.   After about three minutes, he moved into his next phase.

"Now that security needs are changing at rapid rates, it is imperative to find someone who can keep up with the ever evolving realm of national security.   Terrorist are going to new lengths to threaten the well-being of this country.   They hate our freedom." This would be the most ironic thing Gordon would say all night.   It was this coined phrase during his presidential campaign that darted him to the top and practically won him the election.   It was the established explanation to why nations hated America—*because Americans had freedom.*   Hey, Americans believed it, so he went with what worked.   Somehow, the saying "they hate our freedom" rationalized all the terrorist harboring countries' hatred for the American people.   The president knew the real reason as to why certain Middle Eastern regimes attacked superpowers, which was why he was a member of the Baricon, the infamous "terrorist" organization.

Gordon continued, "And because they hate our freedom, they want nothing more than our annihilation.   I don't have to go into the whole *shpill* for you.

"Parnell wasn't helping the country.   He wasn't all there— you've seen him.   He was the most random, mood-swinging, confusing Council member probably in the history of the White House.   He was too stubborn to know when to quit, and to keep him from embarrassing me and allowing for a stupid, avoidable terrorist attack because of his ineffectiveness, I decided to force his retirement.   It was for the protection of you, our family, our friends, all the children of our nation.   We want to provide and ensure a world that the American people can prosper in without the fear of terrorism.   We want a country with an abundance of life, joy, freedom.   Parnell was a threat within himself."

So, the president hit on the emotional appeal aspect and touched on the weaknesses of the old "chap." Now, it was time to move into the kicker: the point that would drive it all home. Gordon went on, "Are you familiar with the Baricon?"

Pamela nodded. She knew what it was. During campaign season, Gordon's pursuit of this regime's obliteration was one of his major platforms. It was not that he was trying to evade them, like former presidents, but rather completely destroy and wipe them into a state of complete powerlessness, which distinguished him. He helped pass a substantial amount of legislature while he was in the US Senate, which was very effective in shutting down these organizations' operations. They complied so easily with American requests while he was leading the US Senate in dealing with terrorist activists from abroad, almost too compliant. This was, of course, because he was a member of the Baricon and the organization reserved certain perks for members moving up to become president of the most powerful country in the world. It was all a set-up, and the rest of the world didn't see it. The president was very manipulative, but he had to be that way in this game. It was for the safety of mankind.

He continued his "*shpill*" carrying on the kicker. "It was brought to my attention by my secret intelligence team that a month ago Parnell had accepted bribes from the Baricon in a counter-intelligence matter. It's almost unbelievable. He has been secretly transmitting some pretty heavy, classified information to them concerning the new defense satellite to be launched next year." This was true, every word of it, but it was still all part of the ultimate set-up. Parnell was a puppet and he walked easily into the trap set in place by Mr. Wade and the Baricon themselves.

The effect this had on Mrs. Wade was beautiful, Gordon noticed. She gasped in shock and absolute awe, unable to utter a single syllable of any word. She tried to reach for words but was entirely unsuccessful as she was utterly flabbergasted by what Gordon had just told her. After moments of attempts to form English words, she finally conceived some type of incoherent gibberish. At the moment she caught her words, she shrieked out a "*What?!*"

Gordon nodded as though thoroughly disappointed at the old chap. "Yes, dear, I can't believe it, either. I really didn't want to mention it. When my secret intelligence team discovered all the details and gathered evidence about his release of the classified satellite blueprints, we substituted most of the content in which he was secretly transmitting to the Baricon with false documents detailing bogus plans. We did this so we could both mislead the receivers and buy time to find out who they were. It was top priority to find out exactly who was receiving the information that Parnell was conveying. We learned that the people being provided this information were the Baricon leaders in Iraq and Pakistan."

"Why didn't you expose him once you found out who he was sending information to?"

"My secret intelligence team and I contemplated it, but decided that it wouldn't be necessarily the most prominent idea. The rationale was simple. If the media was given word that the nation's Central Intelligence Advisor was involved in acts related to treason, it would undoubtedly make the entire White House look unstable. People would be skeptical. Now, this early in my term, is not the time for that." More rambling by Gordon followed. It was a poetic art. The words flowed just right. Words of oratory circumvention: They may have sounded shaky on paper, but conversationally they were as convincing as ever.

Pamela was still in shock, and to annul this shock was an objective that Gordon wanted to accomplish. For she was vulnerable at this stage, so this was the perfect time for him to make the move. He stood behind her with his hands holding hers in front of her body. He whispered the notorious sweet nothingness into her ear.

Alia iacta est.

CHAPTER III

Assassination was illegal, but that was not the sole reason the president had not decided to have Parnell killed before his forced retirement. It was merely for Gordon's false façade of White House perfection. In fact, the aspect of assassination being illegal played such a miniscule role in his decision as that of a particle of snow having an effect on the appearance of Mount Everest's summit.

In (secret) American history, if problems were viewed as a fatal threat to the well-being of the US Government or political interests, government officials sometimes bent the rules and obeyed the 11th Commandment: don't get caught. All sins were thus cleansed if the 11th Commandment was followed. Many unsolved murder cases could thus be traced back to the US Government or a particular party within the government, and the common question of "*who done it?*" could be answered. Many historians have stated that the culprit of such ordered assassinations like that of JFK or Martin

Luther King could be traced back to the governing body of the victims' country of origin. Accounts of history would not mention these occurrences; however, the past would. But in contrast to accounts of history, the past's plea of the truth is a silent scream that does not always reach the ears of future humanity. Accounts of history are biased; on the other hand, the past (or rather, "the truth") is not.

* * *

The currently retired Central Intelligence Advisor was seated at a bar called the Emerald Pub staring at a glass of vodka when Patrick saw him for the first time. Patrick had arrived after being summoned eighteen hours prior to his current undertaking. This undertaking was the stealth assassination of Robert Parnell. Patrick was very pale as if his skin had never been subject to a single sunray. He looked about thirty-five and he was developing a color scheme of gray in his golden hair. There were about sixty strands of gray, which would be approximately one strand per murder, give or take a few. Give a few would probably be the safer bet. If the profession of assassination was baseball, he'd be in the Major Leagues. In fact, he'd be the Babe Ruth, the *Big Bambino* of the game, a curse that had stats consisting of an immense number of hits under his belt.

He was seated across the room from Parnell in a corner looking at an Emerald Pub menu, not really choosing a meal but studying his prey. Every move his prey made was noted. Every word was remembered. Everything was taken in by Patrick who was using all of his acquired knowledge about Parnell in his consideration of his ultimate objective. There was no rush, because one could not rush greatness at work. Like politics was for President Wade, assassination was for Patrick. He was preparing to compose one of his greatest dark compositions to date in his artistic genre, and Parnell (or rather, the sitting duck) was oblivious to the hit man.

Even given the fact of Parnell's apparent unawareness, Patrick maintained his strict method of approach. These codes consisted of attention to detail, obtainment of access, and incognito demeanor. There were many other parts to this code; these three points were the basic essence and the cause of his murderous occupational success.

Parnell ordered another shot of vodka and seemed to be drifting into the realm of a vodka buzz. He was loose with his arms, swinging one when he used his other extremity to drink; and his head stayed down. He appeared to be in a realm of a depressive buzz. Drinking was no real normality for the old, pink-slipped chap but this was a special occasion! The Baricon would surely find out soon, if they had not already, Parnell thought, taking another shot of vodka. The drink's alcoholic proof of eighty was easing the pain. Parnell knew he had some answering to do. Make that a whole lot of answering to do. He would have especial fun in explaining where the Baricon's down payment went. That would be a bunch of laughs...or maybe not. It would be so funny that it would hurt, so hysterical that he would probably cry, and so comical that it might actually kill him. Parnell took yet another hit, and took this one faster than any of the previous four shot glasses. Patrick was still watching, still plotting the assassination. He was watching very closely, in fact. If they taught assassination in high school, Patrick would have had every college on the globe sending him letters of intent for his enrollment at their schools. He wouldn't need it though, because he had already obtained his license to kill though his numerous assassinations. And it was now time for him to exercise the rights explicit in his license. He kept watching, and he never got tired of it. Patrick was getting paid in the seven digits for this. He wasn't doing this for fun anymore.

The sick thrill he once got had vanished ten murders ago in Tijuana. He decided he'd quit after this last high-pay hit on Parnell.

One thing about Patrick was that he never underestimated his prey, not even Parnell, who could be killed at this very moment via a quick knife-slice. Knives weren't the Patrick's preference. He had a passion for creative killings. Simplicity was for another profession. His self-proclaimed art of precision warranted complexity. It had to be intricate or it would not be a "Patrick murder." None of his killings were ever solved with the correct cause of death...ever. He always manipulated his dead prey so that investigation authorities and forensic specialist could not trace anything to him or the party in which he represented. Once in Los Angeles, he walked into his target's home, pointed a gun, pulled the trigger of a no-bullet pop pistol, and scared the old man to death...literally. The forensic report read that the cause of death was a cardiac arrest caused by the man's clogged arteries. No suspicion, no questions, and no evidence left behind were what he left every time. Anyway else would have been entirely too sloppy to him. Sloppiness...special measures were taken to avoid it.

Again, as kooky as it may sound, he considered himself an artist. To himself, he was truly an artist by definition, but he had long lost his passion for the art, yet he never lost that great passion for money. He would betray if necessary. His family tree probably consisted of Judas, Brutus, and Benedict Arnold themselves (probably from his mother's side).

Many would find it interesting that the mass murderer, who was Patrick, was raised by two loving parents, oddly enough. They could possibly have been too adoring of him, if that is possible. They were financially broke, however. Little Patrick needed money. He couldn't afford college so he went to the Army where he learned to shoot and where he committed his first murder. The forensic report read that his commander died of heat stroke. That was true, because his commander did, but they missed the fact that he was tied up inside a small car during a hot summer in Cuba for ten hours before drowning in his own sweat. There was also the guy from Milwaukee, the one from Cleveland, one in Pittsburgh, two in Paris, ten in New York, eight in Seattle, eleven at the same time in Buenos Aires, four in Mexico city...the list went on. If chasing a car over a cliff, which just looked like a steep hill, counted as a murder, then he committed two murders in Colorado.

Parnell was on his ninth shot of his potent beverage when it seemed as though he was in that get-things-together, ready-to-leave mode. Noticing Parnell's drunken shift in interest from the shot glasses, Patrick decided it was time to leave, also. Patrick noticed that the old drunk was not moving at the most rapid pace, so he decided to go ahead and follow the compulsory routine and plant the tracking device on Parnell's car. He walked over to what was identified as the highly intoxicated chap's vacant car and peered inside for a moment. It was rather neat inside, well kept. The black BMW was clean; too bad it wouldn't be maintaining its pretty structure for too much longer, Patrick thought. What a bummer. He looked back inside the glass windows of the bar where Parnell was still drunkenly moping around in, and planted the magnetic device under the passenger side of Parnell's car. The assassin's designed explosive show was to be nothing near anti-climatic, in fact it would be a very attention-grabbing "incident." But it wasn't show time quite yet, so keeping a good eye out was mandatory at this point because initial plans occasionally changed. This was a new method, and Patrick felt a hint of excitement. The same thing over and over again just wasn't ringing his bell anymore. Perhaps, it was to shake things up a bit for his last hit. Thought, tact, and the ethics of assassination were highly regarded, always.

After placing the device, he looked up to find Parnell exiting the bar, wobbling and stutter-stepping all the way into a light pole on the side of the street. This guy was exceedingly inebriated. By the time Parnell was sitting in his rental, Patrick was completely out of the picture, or so it appeared. With frustration, Parnell looked for his keys, which he was unknowingly holding in his hands. After about two minutes of searching for them, he became even more frustrated when he found them gripped tightly in his right hand.

Patrick was patient, so there wasn't even an itch to hit and run (a rookie move). One reason would be because that action would be entirely too sloppy and simple—a big no-no when it came to Patrick. The second reason was that a hit and run at this stage would provide for a way too simple of a forensics expert to determine how Mr. Parnell died. The third, and the most important reason, was the cop car parked two cars down trying to catch speeders. Patrick liked to steer clear of the police. Well, except in Mexico, because there were several crooked cops open to payoffs to overlook something or arrest someone for anything from vagrancy to pushing a shopping cart off the premises of a grocery store parking lot. The police there could be worked with and bribed easily.

Parnell drove off now, into what could have been called "the moonset" because the moon was notably large. Patrick knew where Parnell stayed, so he did not have to follow him closely. Plus, the tracking device was serving its purpose effectively. This kill wouldn't take more than three days, he thought to himself. Well, at least Patrick didn't think it would. Maybe, with the way Parnell was driving, a big ditch or another car driving the opposite direction would do the job for him. If only he could be so lucky. A seven digit paycheck wasn't bad for an unfortunate accident.

Of course, in Parnell's drunken mental state, there had to be an extra stop along the path home. This stop was called the Platinum Lace. The strip club's owner didn't call it a strip club, because those words would be understating the tastefulness and elegance of the place. The owner rather called the strip club an "adult entertainment bar."

The old chap walked into the strip club and was immediately engulfed by an environment full of unclothed women, laser lights, and beer. Ten minutes later, Patrick also made an entrance. The Platinum Lace was the most prestigious place a young lady could make a living in the field of exotic dance. The hiring manager performed his duty with precision and a high level of selectivity. The strip club was very similar in comparison to politics. It was the US Senate of strip clubs; and if a girl was elected into office here, there were a couple of promises. One: fifty thousand a year would be a walk in the park for her, or perhaps a swing down a pole. Two: the strip club would own her soul until they said stop clapping it and start packing it. All of the women learned the hustle well enough to perform after two months as a beer waitress, walking around half naked serving drinks. It gave the women an opportunity to learn the walk, the talk, and how to get paid.

Politics was similar to strip clubs in that politicians learned the ropes and the connections necessary to gain what the game of politics was all about—money. The strippers were vultures; they'd find the rich crowds and flock to them. The other crowds could simply watch from a distance. In a very similar way, politicians, whether Democrat or Republican, would find the rich crowds and flock to them. In the strip club game, or game of the "adult entertainment bars," when a new guy or group of guys walked in, one of the most beautiful and seductive women would walk over and see if he or they wanted a lap dance in the back VIP Room. The cost was usually forty bucks for two songs. The man would either go for it, bargain, suggest a dance later, or decline (declining to the stripper's offer usually as politely as manly possible). There was never any negotiation on price but always a mandatory giggle and tease on the stripper's part as a part of professional courtesy. Ten minutes later, he or they would be approached again. If a decline was made again, that was the last offer of the night unless he or they went up to the center stage and start throwing down immense amounts of paper with presidents' faces on them. The strip club was very comparable in relation to the political game: special favors were always up for grabs if an individual had the money.

In politics, if a politician knew the hustle, a politician would get to know the money. The way it all worked was very meticulous and the game was very uniform. The strip club hustle was the same in uniformed code. For example, at the Platinum Lace, since there was one main stage in the center and two cylinder stages in the corners, called satellites, each girl had to do three stage dances every two hours. In total, three dances would last approximately twelve to fifteen minutes. The profit made while on the stages ranged from two hundred to four hundred dollars a night. The remainder of the time was spent sitting on laps of the rich and wealthy which made a reasonable amount of money, and lap dancing in the VIP Room which earned between three hundred and six hundred a night. All together, a stripper working at the Platinum Lace could make over a thousand dollars on a good night. Good nights included Fridays, Saturdays, and work holidays. Every stripper also had to pay nightly rent to the owner which came out to a hundred bucks on weekends and fifty on weekdays. The strip club was a very profitable business much like politics.

Parnell stumbled in and sat in one of the snug sofa seats near a corner halfway between one of the satellites and the main stage. In his drunkenness, he made quite the selection on seats because his point of view wasn't bad given the crowdedness of the club on this particular night. He had a clear vista of the stripper on center stage as well as the strippers in both satellites. Immediately upon seating himself, a beautifully slender woman with a push-up bra, robust breasts, and a thong approached him.

She leaned over him and whispered, "Hey, baby, my name is Gracie. I would *love* to get to know you a little better in the back."

Parnell smiled widely, as her hand slid from his shirt to his trousers, and said, "I would *love* to get to know you, too. Whatever you're charging for the back, I'll double it." He was now in the game. She enthusiastically obliged his offer as she grabbed his hand very excitedly and led him to the VIP Room—everywhere a reluctantly retired, old man would want to be. There was a light-up sign near one of the back corners which read "VIP Room." Parnell was thinking of it more as an exalted "Paradise."

The assassin watched the entire thing from across the room. Despite the abundance of beautiful, naked women swarming the place, Patrick was focused on his prey. Here, there was a one drink minimum, so Patrick had a Smirnoff in his hand, but he did not indulge. Alcohol was for his prey. He believed that in order to commit the perfect murders, one must be alcoholically unspoiled. His prey and the environment around him were his only concern.

At this point, Parnell, the old chap, was having the time of his life. He left the VIP Room (or his "Paradise") with an ear-to-ear smile on his face. He was ecstatic and overly inebriated. After about an hour of standing around center stage putting dollar bills between his lips and letting strippers take his money with theirs mouths, Parnell had seen enough XXX content to last a lifetime.

It was now time for the drunken patsy and old chap to depart and call it a night. He was about fifteen to twenty minutes away from home as he pulled out of the parking lot of the Platinum Lace.

He swerved over into other cars' lanes as he erroneously drew nearer to his home. Like any good assassin would do, Patrick was a few cars behind in his Infiniti G35, staying a lane or two over, not attracting any attention. Parnell was sitting at a red light, after about ten minutes of driving, still fifteen or twenty minutes away from his house. Still at the red light, he pressed on the gas and the brake simultaneously, enjoying the emanation of the *Vrrrooom* sound from his BMW. The light turned green at the intersection, and Parnell sped off quickly, then immediately stopped—this sudden stopping in the middle of the road was, of course, not caused by anything other than the drunken Parnell's will to stop at that moment, randomly. A car traveling directly behind him honked loudly as it had to sharply swerve to avoid hitting Parnell's BMW from the back. Hearing the honk, Parnell gave a louder, longer honk back. Then, as the car was speeding up in the other lane next to Parnell, he rolled down his window and stuck his head as far out of the car as he could while still keeping his foot on the pedal and yelled, "*Honk! Honk! Honkeedy! Honk! Honk!*" Then, he nicked his head on the top of the door as he moved his head back into the car. He rolled up his window and watched as the car drove off speedily into the distance.

Parnell thought about chasing after the car, but he decided he would much rather sing a song. He sang to a joyfully slurred tune, "Honk! Honk! Honkeedy! Honk!" He sang and ran a stop sign all at once. Seeing the stop sign as he was passing it, he immediately stopped his car in the middle of the intersection. Realizing his fault, he put the car in reverse and drove his car backwards so that he could correct his wrong and stop at the sign. He drove recklessly once again after pausing for the sign. He was like a teenager under the false self-assurance of self-immortality, which was a rare character trait of older people. He had never broken a bone in his life, and he had very rare incidences of physical bodily afflictions even though he had served in the military for several years. His luck, as far as his physical health was concerned, was about to end. His mental health had already done so.

Parnell swerved and randomly slammed on his brakes all the way home. In approximately forty minutes after his leave from the Platinum Lace, he finally arrived at his home. Now, it was time to deal with Mrs. Parnell. Perhaps the reason Parnell's once brilliant military and strategic mind had gone away (forever) was partially (or fully) because of the long marriage to the lady the neighbors called simply "The Witch." Without a shadow of a doubt, she would be up, widely wakeful upon his entry into the house. She would be there to nag, and Parnell was happy to be drunk. The hangover in the morning would be well worth not comprehending an ounce of what the old lady would be yapping about when he got in. He stumbled into the house; she yelled and yapped; he laughed at his own joke about her needing an ironing board to straighten out some wrinkles on her unsightly face. This made her yell more, and Parnell passed out in their bed, perfectly content, as his assassin eased past the drunken chap's house, adding notes into his Blackberry phone.

CHAPTER IV

"Good morning, Mr. Hataki. How are you?" Patrick asked casually.

"Hi, Roy, I'm hoping for good news from you today. Will the job be done within the next two days?"

"Yes, Mr. Hataki," Patrick confirmed as the other end of the line simultaneously disconnected. Hearing the humming from the other end, Patrick hung up the pay phone. Then, he left the colorfully arranged children's section of the DC main library. As he was exiting the library, a young girl of no more than five or six years of age, wearing a little blue dress with a notably large head, approached behind Patrick. She tugged on the tail of his overcoat as she came to the halt of her frolicked skipping. Immediately, Patrick whipped around out of militant habit to confront the unknown assailant. She immediately ran off. Seeing the girl, Patrick paused for a moment, and then went about his stroll. He sat in his car and arrived at an unanticipated epiphany: His phone was missing.

He put his car keys back into his pocket, opened the driver door, and pulled the tail of his sweater to straighten it out a bit. He arose from the car in the parking lot and was pissed-off but intensely calculating at the same time. The phone was very important, especially today (and not only because he had free weekend minutes). He walked back into the library, probing. He needed to get that phone. He looked over each book shelf, searching for the young girl in the blue dress. An instant realization occurred to Patrick. There was a bigger picture to the puzzle than a little thief who had an occupation of stealing cell phones in local libraries. It was highly implausible that she could have been alone. She wasn't just a big-headed girl skipping around. She had not just been a singular thief—she was too young and too small. *Had someone caught on*, wondered Patrick. Everything now was a little more complicated. Patrick paced himself through the quick fleetness of the moments as he desperately but collectively attempted to keep his composure while searching for his vital necessity. He walked over to one of the library assistants working at the center desk of the children's library.

"Excuse me, miss. Have you seen a small girl with a blue dress and black hair around here?"

The librarian looked at Patrick for a moment, apparently accessing her brain's memory bank for a small girl in a blue dress with black hair. Then, arriving at a place of remembrance, she answered, "Yes, are you referring to the young girl that was skipping all over the library? By the way, this is a library, not a zoo."

"Yes, that's the one," Patrick said with a casual tone as if the girl was his niece or something.

"Yes sir, she skipped out the back entrance a minute or so ago. Do you see that door those guys in the suits are exiting out of in the back?"

Hearing this, Patrick immediately peered towards the back of the library where the "Exit" sign glowed red. He then started walking quickly toward the door, leaving the librarian with a very perplexed look on her face. He walked faster. A young teen was walking a perpendicular path and was knocked over by the momentum of the striding assassin. Papers flew up into the air. This library pedestrian accident was simply disregarded by Patrick as his only focus was on the door. He took a quick turn onto the book aisle were the back exit was located. He shoved the door open and was simultaneously blinded by the brightness of the outside. He then heard a skid of wheels and a vehicle speed off. He put his left hand over his eyes, shielding them from the sun. As his eyes adjusted, the assassin spotted a black Avalanche pull out of the now vacant back parking lot. Patrick reacted quickly as he started to run around the building through the grass towards his car. Watching the black Avalanche speeding off, he ran parallel to the SUV's driving route.

The Avalanche sped down the road quickly and consequently was flagged down by the sirens of a police car as it approached an upcoming intersection. Simply, it was Patrick's luck. Patrick saw this and concurrently started his rental G35. He put his right hand behind the passenger seat of the car, looked back, and sped in reverse out of his spot. Then, he swiftly switched the gear into drive and spun the car out of the lot. He grabbed the car phone that was resting next to him. He punched in the numbers to get in touch with Vice President Lannigan.

"Hataki speaking," answered Vice President Lannigan.

"Mr. Hataki, this is Roy," said Patrick.

"Hello, Roy. Where are you?"

"It seems that someone has been watching me. I have reason to believe that my phone has been stolen."

"Where are you?"

"In my car."

"Do you know who may have stolen it?

"No."

"That's not good."

"I had some of my personal information on the phone: phone numbers, credit card numbers, and some pictures."

"Does it have a GPS locator?"

"Of course not."

"You need to recover that phone. It seems that it is very important to you. If it fell into the wrong hands, the consequences could be pretty bad. Is the information protected?"

"Yes."

"That gives you time. You need to retrieve your phone by any means possible, as soon as possible. I don't care what you have to do. That is a direct order. I want no traces. Call me when you do." And, with that, the conversation was concluded.

Patrick (Roy, when he was talking to Vice President Lannigan a.k.a. Mr. Hataki) pulled over into the McDonald's parking lot across the street to watch the SUV while it was pulled over to the side. He quickly figured that if the police officer dismissed the moving violation once the officer learned of the identity and affiliation of the men in the Avalanche, the men were likely to be officers or agents of some local or federal agency. He was hoping that this would not be the case. The officer approached the Avalanche and Patrick's worst fear was confirmed. They had badges, obviously; their moving violation was excused as the police officer did not write the ticket and got back in his squad car to catch his next moving violator. This was revealing. Patrick might have been better off if he smoked Parnell the Patsy yesterday.

The Avalanche was now pulling off the side of the street and speeding once again through the intersection. Patrick, with the accompaniment of his assassin instinct decided that it would be the preeminent idea to find out exactly who these guys were. He knew that he probably wasn't going to get his phone back as quietly as he wanted. His next move would not be his own decision but the decision of Vice President Lannigan whom had given him the direct order. Usually, he would not have even thought about causing a scene, as he realized he had to do, but he cared enough about his own life preservation to do so. Retrieval of his phone was essential to his survival. Patrick sped out of the McDonald's parking lot he had pulled over into, and proceeded on to the grand, new operation of recovering his phone.

He sped up to them, letting them know that he was, in fact, following them. Patrick put his right blinker on and merged over into the lane directly left of the Avalanche. The two vehicles were now parallel, going about fifty-five mph down 15th Street. Seeing that Patrick had no weapon in his hands and showing their own guns for Patrick to see in case he wanted to try anything involving gun-play, the Avalanche driver let down his window. Patrick let his window down and politely asked the Avalanche's occupants for his phone back.

As unforeseeable as it may have seemed, the driver did not oblige (as if they didn't have the slightest idea what Patrick was talking about). Patrick rolled up his window, as he had new enthusiasm now. All it took to bring out the cold-blooded murderer in Patrick was polite disagreement. Patrick decided to take the driver's comment personally. He resolved now that he was going to get his phone back on this street. Reality still held that the task be highly unlikely, but he determined that reality was to be defied on this particular occasion. Patrick looked at the Avalanche and shook his head out of pity. The situation was about to get really ugly. But this was okay with Patrick who lived a life under the aphorism that if one is to go out, one should go out in flames. The fire was right next to Patrick there in the Avalanche and the flames were about to be unleashed.

Patrick slammed on the gas and whipped the steering wheel to the right so that his car swerved into the black SUV. At this moment, anger clouded his mind and infuriated passion filled his heart, (that is, if he had one). He darted his car into the Avalanche's left side repeatedly, creating pretty sizable indentions on the SUV. Noticing the low population density of the street, Patrick sped to 70 mph, going ahead of the Avalanche. He pulled the lever to initiate the emergency break and turned the car ninety degrees, stopping ten meters in front of the Avalanche. The driver of the Avalanche slammed on the brake as the SUV crashed into the passenger side of Patrick's car at about fifteen miles an hour. Patrick's air bag then inflated into his face. Seeing nothing but the white from the airbag, he unbuckled his seatbelt and exited his vehicle (Oh, the safety features of modern day, Patrick thought). He was still consumed by his fuming anger as he walked over to the presently immobilized Avalanche without a single thought of what he was going to do. As he did this, guns were pulled from the waistlines of three men who occupied the crashed and halted Avalanche. Before they could tell Patrick to freeze, Patrick retreated from his stance and dropped quickly to a rapid rolling motion on the asphalt. He grabbed his gun from his waist and, without a second thought, did what any best assassin in the world would do in his position: impulsively open-fired. One down, two down, three suited men down, and altogether this occurred in less than a fifteen second span. The only agent or officer, or whatever they were, that was left was the girl standing behind the wrecked SUV. Then, she started shooting through the windows of the vehicle. What kind of little girl in a blue dress was this? Patrick shot at her shooting arm, accurately hitting his aimed target. As she dropped her weapon, Patrick raced over and with one swipe pistol-whipped her unconscious. He picked her up, carried her inside the Avalanche, and threw her into the back seat. He was still heated, but the cognitive wheels in his mind were moving more quickly now. Concurrently, he refused to allow his anger to take over at this point. It was now time to think smart for the escape as opposed to passionately, as he did during the actual killing part of all of his assassinations. It was also the time to think quickly, because law enforcers were soon to be present, and car traffic had already stopped along with hysterically yelling standby pedestrians. He looked on the passenger seat and saw his Blackberry phone.

He looked at one of the dead men that he shot, lying face up and lifeless on the pavement and said, "You should have given me my cell phone when I asked for it the first time." At the same time as he was saying this, he heard the sirens. Patrick swiftly jumped into the Avalanche, backed the truck up, and exited the scene. Then, he looked into the rearview and saw a police car about twenty meters directly behind him. He heard some kind of gibberish that was coming from the officer's car, but he did not feel it was necessarily relevant enough at the time to actually listen to what the officer was saying. He figured that it was something like "pull over!" or at least something to that effect. In the assassin's mind, the stopping-the-car notion was the farthest thing from his top priority. As his head operated in overload, balancing instinct and thorough cognizant reasoning, he found himself hanging a right turn off of 15th Street onto Houston Street. At that time, he was accompanied by another patrol car. This police car's occupant was yelling out something like

"Stop your vehicle!" or something similar in sound, also. Did they really expect the guy who just killed three men, kidnapped a small, big-headed girl, and stole an SUV to stop as a result of their police command? Probably not, but it can be supposed that they figured that they might as well give it a try.

Focusing on several things at once, Patrick found himself deleting everything in his cell phone. Most of it was committed to his memory anyway. The phone was merely back-up. After deleting the memory, he took both hands off the steering wheel to use them as leverage to break the Blackberry in half. His mission had now been accomplished and all evidence was destroyed.

He now found himself on the expressway. This day was just getting greater and greater with every moment. At least he had a hostage, he figured. As all of this was happening, something else came to pass, unfortunately for him. One flat tire, two flat tires, and Patrick felt his car come to a sojourn. Maybe it could have gotten worse. Patrick tried to think of how it could have and came to the supposition that the police officers could have flattened his other two tires, which would have thus theoretically made the situation much worse, perhaps. He thought about getting out of the car and putting his hands up—the whole surrendering thing—but that wasn't his nature. So, he decided that he would sit inside and patiently wait to be retrieved by the officers that so nicely flattened the tires of his stolen Avalanche.

The passenger doors were being opened as Patrick didn't give the two officers standing outside the door the pleasure of a response or acknowledgement of any kind.

"Please step outside the vehicle and put your hands up free of any objects!" one of the officers commanded with a tone of firm authority. Patrick wasn't budging; they'd be carrying him out, surely. They asked, or told, him again. As a result, he again remained in defiance to their orders. They, in result, released him of his duty to sit in the driver's seat. Patrick found himself in an awkward position as he was thrown out of the car. He stared at the grains of concrete laying on the street pavement alongside his face. Surely, he could report this as an instance of immoral police brutality. Surely, all of this roughness and such wasn't called for even given the fact Patrick had a gun, stole a car, shot three men, kidnapped a big-headed girl, and resisted arrest. He attempted, without any gain, to escape the holds of the officers that were detaining him on the ground. He kicked his legs with no effectiveness. He tried to swing his arms but was penned down to the point that the only moving part his body that was allowed to move was his heart and toes. He tried to pull off the impossible task of raising himself up from the oppression of the five police officers that were penning him down. He again struggled to move and refused to go to jail without a fight. It was hopeless, however, and Patrick knew his struggling would result in no actual achievement of any kind other than make his bail out of jail more impossible than it already was. The next thing he knew, he was hearing his Miranda rights.

"You are under arrest by the DC Police Department, and it my duty to advise you of your constitutional rights. You have the right to remain silent. If you give up the right to remain silent, anything you say will be used against you in the court of law. You have the right to talk to a lawyer before any questioning and to have one with you during questioning, if you wish. If you cannot afford a lawyer, one will be appointed to you by the court before any questioning. Do you understand these rights?"

Gazing at the asphalt roadway, Patrick took his head and busted it on the ground. He wasn't quite losing his mind; he figured they couldn't send him to jail unconscious. The throbbing and loud ringing in his head ignited excruciating pain, but Patrick did it again, this time harder. He figured he would act as a masochist and abuse himself more as if he was receiving pleasure from his self-abuse. He dropped his head on the pavement and was finally out cold.

The police picked the motionless body off the ground, handcuffed Patrick, and called for an ambulance. Meanwhile, two officers were in the back of the Avalanche with the kidnapped girl, trying to bring her into consciousness. They were unsuccessful; Patrick had hit a point in her head just right so that she wouldn't be waking up any time soon. Two other officers were standing near the right shoulder of the expressway. One of the officers looked at another officer and said, "What a sick bastard—tried to kill himself."

The other officer shook his head and said, "Well, he wasn't successful. They ought to give this guy the chair."

"Why did he kill those guys over on Alabama and 15th?"

"I haven't heard anything. He's probably insane. They are over there with the kidnapped lady now. She must be a dwarf of something because they just got an ID off her that says she's DIA."

"The DIA? This definitely wasn't some random thing."

"They never are."

"What do you mean?"

"Killings, whether it's a serial killer or an assassin doing it, are very rarely a random thing. The killers usually always know who they're killing. I don't care what those physiologist pricks say at the department."

"Man, this world gets crazier and crazier everyday. I can't even let my little girl ride the school bus without wondering if the bus driver is a child molester."

"You never know nowadays."

"The three other guys that he shot—were they in the DIA?"

"I wouldn't doubt it. It was like a gun standoff. The paperwork on this should be just great." Both cops sighed and walked over to the crazed man that they had been chasing. The ambulances had arrived and the crazed Patrick was lifted up into an emergency vehicle. The two officers followed the ambulance that was transporting Patrick to the hospital. They would have to stand post until the jailers from the city jail came to the hospital to watch him. The way he was looking, he would be in the hospital awhile.

Once at the hospital, they pushed the comatose Patrick over to the emergency room on a stretcher so that his open wounds on his busted head could be closed because he was bleeding profusely. They identified that Patrick had a TBI, traumatic brain injury, with low-level obtundation. He was stone cold, but alive, and was only responsive to painful stimulation. His pupil dilation test showed that his pupils were abnormally dilating indicated brain injury, so the nurses sent him over to have a CT Scan. In reality, he wasn't as unconscious as he was pretending to be. He knew what measures they would go about to make certain hospital prisoners weren't fabricating the truth of their actual unconsciousness so they could stay in the hospital longer than they needed. One of the nurses said "Ammonia capsule," and Patrick began to immediately breathe slower. From his working knowledge of chemical substances, he knew that Ammonia capsules were exposed under patients' noses to reveal if the hospital prisoners were truly unresponsive or not. In order to avoid coughing and sputtering once the capsule was placed under his nose, which would prove he was faking his consciousness level, Patrick was breathing very slowly in shallow breaths. If he was to breathe normally, it would be impossible to hold out from sharing his true state of growing consciousness with the nurses though his consequent air gagging and such caused by the capsule. Luckily, he withheld from reacting to the chemical and passed the Ammonium capsule test.

He had an awfully loud ringing in his head, but that would only classify him as being in the state of confused delirium and that would not keep him out of the dreaded jail for long. He knew he would have to fake his unconsciousness well, because the Baricon might have a little difficulty helping him in jail. The chance of extradition would be much greater from a guarded hospital room rather than the alternative.

He was stripped of his clothes and put in a green hospital gown. Once it was established that Patrick was not critical, they placed him under care to be examined. The CT Scan was negative, showing that he did not have a brain disorder. The doctor's visit was short. There was the usual check of heart rate, but Patrick remained persistent in his act as an unconscious patient and was true to the end.

Patrick had a history of faking ailments. When he was in junior high school, back when the little assassin was a preteen, he did a full fledge study on the symptoms of pink eye and shammed his way out the classroom, to the nurse's office, to the back seat of his mother's car on the way home. Simply by applying pressure to his eye when he went to the restroom and complaining to the optometrist of a sticky feeling when he closed his eyelids, young Patrick was set to take useless medications and stay out of school. Pink eye was a hideous epidemic, Little Patrick dramatically showed with his faked eye ailment.

Back to the present, while he was laying across the examination table, being randomly poked by the doctor, he thought to himself that maybe he should have pulled that old trick of pink eye instead of injuring himself by banging his head on the highway pavement earlier in the day. The doctor said some medical gibberish to some young lady, and she was thoroughly concurring with his observations in an overly assertive manner (Patrick concluded she was probably a med school student). He lay lifeless some more until the doctor stopped writing and talking and, finally, left the room.

The ringing in his head had gone down a bit. The drugs that he was given upon his arrival to the hospital were setting in to subdue the painful throbbing in his head. He felt better but he slightly wished that the agony would return to its full sensation to make his faked state of unconsciousness easier to fake and more believable to the hospital staff.

Handcuffed to his bed in a four-point lock with both arms and legs chained to the bed, Patrick began to once again plot, but was constantly interrupted by the ringing in his head. Complete thoughts were interrupted by throbs in his head from his earlier self-affliction and medical drugs which the nurses kept coming in and injecting into him.

He could hear the police officers conversing outside in the hall about the occurrences of the day. It was interesting to Patrick to listen to them discuss whether he should get capital or not. They thought his name was Robert Smith—the Baricon had provided quite the convincing fake identification cards and passports. One of the officers was nice enough to say that "Robert" should get the ancient gas chamber for multiple murders and causing his car to skid into a cement barrier getting onto the freeway. The other officers seemed to think that life imprisonment was the most sufficient punishment that any human being could get. These were such nice guys that Patrick hoped that they were around if the Baricon was to indeed come for him. Surely the Baricon would come for him, Patrick thought, because he was now in the hospital with a traumatic brain injury. There's no telling what he would tell in his confused delirium. There was no telling what beans he might drop about his secret assignment. There was no telling what names he could mention. There was no telling how much proof he could provide. Certainly, the Baricon would come for him.

CHAPTER V

Gordon watched the entire gun scene on the news headlining *the unidentified man of middle age who open-fired and killed three DIA officers in Washington at approximately 12:30 this afternoon.* The president rubbed his head and closed his eyes. He thought to himself, "This news coverage was exactly what I need." The assassin, not AN assassin but THE assassin, was supposed to be THE best. Being THE best, a professional, why was THE best killer in the world on the news shooting federal agents? Gordon sat up in his brown leather recliner that he was so comfortably relaxing in while watching the news. He kicked off his alligator boots, pulled off his socks, and put his bare, pedicured feet on his lavish rug and started making fists with his toes on the rug. It was a relaxation exercise—he saw it in a movie before. He did this for a few more moments and then decided to stand up. He relaxed his feet now, liberating his toes from the scrunched position, allowing them to reside in a flat and natural state of being. He stood, and now slowly paced. He didn't usually pace, but what the hay! This was a special occasion! He searched for any humor before he actually sat down and created a plot to fix everything—just another day in the life as president.

He closed his eyes while he was walking and began meditating. As he drew in slow breaths, he also drew a few conclusions. One conclusion was that Patrick would need to disappear. No, not just disappear—he needed to disappear without a trace and very quickly. He needed to be hidden and perhaps killed because now he was no longer part of the solution to the Baricon's problems. He was, at this time, the exact opposite of solving anything. THE best assassin was now THE best problem. Whether Patrick was to live or not was to be decided at a later time. Presently, it was time to figure out how THE best assassin was to be swiftly extradited from the hospital.

* * *

In retrospect and in a broad sense, most of the world agreed with the president's underlying scheme; they just didn't know it. The president and the Baricon believed in the ancient political principle that sometimes in order to produce good, one must participate in evil. Perhaps the measures that the president was executing were not exactly the world's idea of great morality and such, but the president felt that these dishonest measures were necessary for the ultimate good. Many would consider the president's desire to have the patsy Parnell killed gruesomely evil. Many would consider the president's desire to have America's legislative branch crumbled into absolute ineffectiveness shockingly sinister. These very factors were the reasons that the public was not to know of the scheme, now or ever. Similarly, like people never knew of such foul presidential and executive schemes that occurred many time past. They were oblivious because accounts of history never recognized these parts of the past. To Gordon, his scheme would have to be perfectly carried through to carry on the existence of mankind. His underhanded plan was essential for human survival, he believed. He realized that history might never explain what he and the Baricon was planning to accomplish. He figured history might remember him as the worst president to date for what he was about to cause in the world, if his scheme wasn't undertaken with total precision, and he failed to carry out the 11th Commandment. Gordon knew that this would be the hardest task of his life, even harder than the election, which wasn't a walk in the park (especially for an Independent party candidate).

Indeed, in most presidents' careers in the past, the election and campaigning was the most difficult part of their pre-presidential and presidential terms. Gordon did compromise his own sanity at times for plotting what he was going to do for the simple fact that, according to the vast majority of world, his underlying endeavor would be perceived as completely...well...evil. But, sometimes to give great mercy and compassion for those one loves, one must participate in great evil, believed Gordon.   According   to Gordon, evil was merely lack of empathy, or rather empathetic feeling for one's fellow person. He felt that he was extremely compassionate simply for the evil he was scheming to participate in (ironic as it may seem). And, he was truly compassionate by most people's standards. His wife knew, especially. That's why she loved him so much and ever unconditionally. She was that one person who was able to feel the true, genuine heart of Gordon. And he too was in the same love boat. He lied to her, however. He lived a lie in front of her. He hated it, but he did it because he loved her, he kept telling himself. He did it, because she was so precious to him. He would reveal it in time, but until then it was *Alia iacta est*. The dice were always cast; and their marriage was gambled. Knowing this, he seized every opportunity and every moment with her. He held every one of them so dear in his heart. He took in everything from the sweet smell of her hair to the soothing membrane she wore as skin. She was poetry to him. She was inspiration to life! Nevertheless, he had to lie to her.

He reminded himself that it was for her own good. He questioned what would happen over and over...at the end of all this. This world, tainted by weapons of mass destruction, was on a course to self-obliteration, and his scheme was the only way to stop the annihilation of mankind, or so he truly felt. Concerning his supposition, he was not completely wrong, and on paper his scheme seemed to work. She was definitely an obstacle that would stand in the way of the plot. Gordon felt that he was protecting her, protecting the world, protecting... perhaps the future. Or was it himself? Was his intent deep-seeded to selfishness?

* * *

Gordon now had a new problem in his plan. THE best assassin was still THE best obstacle at this moment. Gordon walked over to his desk and pulled up his chair, his favorite chair. He slouched in his presidential brown leather and contemplated his coming moves regarding Patrick. He thought more on this as he made fists with his toes on the carpet beneath his feet. He meditated more, stopped, and then meditated again. There was much riding on this and this fact kept making itself more and more evident as the pendulum swung on the clock across the room. Time was of the essence, especially at this particular time. Decisiveness was definitely in order at this time, but the best decision was at hand, as well. If he was to neglect being decisive, he would be delaying in an emergency situation that would come back to provide quite the catastrophic repercussions. However, if he did not determine the best decision, the consequence would be equally unpleasant. He picked up the phone and decided that it was the preeminent decision—he had to call Vice President Lannigan (or Mr. Hataki as he was called by THE best problem/assassin). Lannigan was in Buenos Aires on his self-proclaimed "strategically arranged" vacation.

"Hey, Lanny, you see the news this evening?" Gordon asked as if he was referring to news concerning a normal daily news matter. President Wade and Vice President Lannigan had been good friends from Columbia University in undergrad and political partners for over twenty years. That's how they were jointly revolutionized by the Baricon philosophy.

They didn't act like the average president-vice president team; they were truly friends. That genuine comradeship had glowed on the screens of millions of television sets during the past election season, thus, creating a major plus in the American vote. They were not the typical Kobe and Shaq team, working well together on the court, but not off. They were more like the Jordan and Pippin partnership, productively achieving in the game as well outside of it. There was no contesting the fact that they were champs in the game of politics. Both could have made it on their own, so jointly they were a rare, great package. After election season, they didn't see each other quite as much due to the fact that executive security made sure the two were separated as much as possible—just in case. In case of what? Basically, in case someone was plotting the same murderous task that they were co-plotting against the ex-intelligence advisor, Robert Parnell—or in a simpler sense: assassination. Unfortunately for them, Parnell was not closer to his ill-fated end. He was still as good as dead though, without a shadow of a doubt. They would surely finish the job, as they had done in the past.

When they had "Baricon discussions" they didn't sound like politicians nor act like them. That was for the political game. The Baricon was much more than a political organization to them. It was a true brotherhood. It was the preservation of mankind, for goodness sake! They were the heroes flying into the hopeless night to save the world from the depths of despair! For all it was, when they talked outside of the political twaddle, they weren't politicians. They were intuitive plotters of the future of all humanity, or so they believed.

They were the major heads of the government, so secure phone lines were provided; they made sure of it. No one would ever hear their conversations. Since President Nixon, every president made absolutely sure that their private conversations could not be recorded or monitored. This aspect of allowing presidents to stonewall their conversations left room for benefit abuse, and not only in the term of President Wade.

"Yes, they have it on CNN looking like a modern version of an old Western," Lannigan responded, rather lightly.

"And this was supposed to be the easy part. Did you talk to him this morning?" Gordon asked this, shifting quickly from sarcasm in his statement to earnest seriousness in his question.

"I talked to him. He stated that the job would be done within two days. I also received a call from him last night. He followed Parnell yesterday evening and today to track the old man and get acquainted with his behaviors," Lannigan said as he sipped on a pina colada thoroughly enjoying his "strategically arranged" vacation on a secluded beach on the outskirts of Buenos Aires.

"All right, we are caught in a bit of a gridlock. We have a man who needs to be taken care of and a man who is now being held in a hospital who is supposed to assassinate the man that's supposed to be taken care of."

"First, I think we need to actually look at what happened and what culminated in that," Lannigan suggested simply, taking another strategically arranged sip of his colada. Everything was "strategically arranged" with Vice President Lannigan, sometimes in actuality, mostly in his own mind.

"Lanny, the thing that brings unease to me is that I haven't received a report from any of the agencies concerning the homicide incident from earlier today. Normally, in a similar scenario I would have been informed promptly," Gordon said with more of a concerned tone as if Lannigan wasn't picking up on the significance of the situation.

"Well, Gordon, we have to ask if this is an emergency that requires that you be promptly notified about. All that has been reported is a random shooting of some federal agents," Lannigan said inattentively as he dabbled his miniature umbrella in his glass.

"Not to be overly pessimistic   regarding our Buffalo Bill shootout remake today, but I would hate to imagine that they would know about the assassination intent," Gordon said, becoming more and more concerned as Lannigan's level of concern seemed to decrease dramatically (along with the amount of colada he had in his glass).

"Look, let's not assume the worst. It—"

"No, we must assume the worst," Gordon interrupted, "always." It was okay that Lannigan was interrupted by Gordon; he wanted another sip of his pina colada, anyway.

There was a brief moment of silence in which both exchanged silent, nonverbal ideas. Gordon spoke first. "In order to get the best result, we have to anticipate the worst possible scenario."

"I agree, but let's not overly preoccupy ourselves with things that we don't need to be too anxious about. It could be nothing," Lannigan brought to mind, looking at his finger tips, the quintessence of the body language expression of relaxed blitheness.

"I don't know what you're doing out there on the beach, but I must ask you to understand the sense of urgency in this matter.

Certainly, this is a simple problem that can be fixed; however, it is still a problem."

"I'll put it this way. All of this is coming to a conclusion very soon. You and I both know we are kings of the world right now. In this country, we control the entity of this great land our forefathers stole from the Indians—excuse me—Native Americans. Not to toot your horn or gas you up, but you are the Commander-in-Chief of the military. Throw your weight around if you want. Pull all the information on this DIA homicide matter. Don't worry too much; everything will be copasetic."

"This could very possibly be a very troubling predicament for us."

As Gordon was saying this, Lannigan was thinking, *here we go again.*

"I haven't received any information concerning Patrick from the DIA, the FBI, anybody. Guy is doing a rendition of the Oklahoma City massacre around DC, kidnapping and killing federal agent. Say you're the head of the agency—who do you inform?"

"Not that simple. It's not just case-closed like that. There are other factors to consider. You don't get presented with information about all the homicides that take place in this country. Think— "

"You're right. But, who was shot by Patrick?"

There was a pause. Lannigan personally thought that it was a rhetorical inquiry. It wasn't. "Three DIA agents," he answered upon his realization that the question was not rhetorical.

"DIA," Gordon echoed.

"Yes, DIA."

"What does that stand for?" Gordon asked with the tone of a school teacher trying to get a kindergartener to read the word "cat" or "dog."

"Okay... Domestic Intelligence Agency," Lannigan said, going along.

"Domestic as in..."

"The US," answered Lannigan clearly seeing where the president was going with this line of semi-rhetorical questioning. "What's your point?"

"A homicide is worked on by local bureaus and law enforcement. When something is a threat to the security of our country who comes in?"

"I see what you're saying. However, I don't think that it's anything to overly worry about or be excessively uneasy over."

"Do you realize— "

This time Lannigan interrupted, "Okay. I don't think you're being paranoid, but I think we need to ponder on this more before we start drawing up hypothetical scenarios. Let's not go too far; that's all I'm saying."

"Well, we know we have the Baricon operatives at our disposal. That brings me a higher level of comfort, but do we take care of him or rescue him...or move him out of the hospital and then take care of him?"

"I propose we independently contemplate for five and get back on the issue."

"Sounds good," Gordon said, hanging up his phone.

Vice President Lannigan was too preoccupied with other things at the time to worry about the state of affairs in the world and so on. Tonight was an important night of his strategically arranged vacation. He was in Buenos Aires sipping on a very potently alcoholic beverage, but in moderation, of course. Later, he would be having one of his "affiliates" coming over to give him a massage. He had not looked forward to such a massage in a long time. Work was all he had been doing for the past several months; there was no time for sleep. It was his chance to unwind. Now, slightly buzzed, feeling absolutely excellent in his buzz, and clouded by the non-caring nature of this beverage, Lannigan laid back in his comfortable bed and flipped on the television. He thought about calling his lady "affiliate" and seeing exactly how far she was away, because this was indeed the most pressing matter on his mind. The DIA shooting—it was important, but it was work. He was on vacation. He decided not to be overly brutal concerning Patrick in having him killed and all because he might regret it later...maybe. He decided that the best thing was to keep him alive for now, and perhaps tomorrow he would make a decision on his fate. His old buddy, Gordon, would be taking care of all that for now.

Up until this vacation, Lannigan would have usually been up contemplating and concerning himself entirely with work, but he had started to notice that it was starting to make him a little crazy. He felt as if his brain was in overload, and that was the reason for the vacation. The bigger—in fact—the biggest fish were to be fried in the very near future, as Lannigan wanted to be fresh for it—fresh for the big show. It would be one of the biggest undertakings in the history of treason. Although, Lannigan also knew that if it were not done properly and down to the letter, history might not mention what they would do in these coming days in the light in which they wished it would be mentioned. This was basically because if they did it wrong, history might end along with the scholars and... humanity as a whole.

Gordon was not having thoughts even similar or close in any proximity to those of his friend Lannigan in Buenos Aires, or "Lanny" as he usually called him. It had been five minutes, and Gordon called him back.

"Call in the Baricon operatives; have them extradite Patrick out of the country by midnight," he said very decisively this time around.

Lannigan nodded as if Gordon could see him and asked, "Where to?"

"Somewhere they can't hear him scream for mercy," Gordon said even more decisively.

"And what about our friend Parnell?"

"He won a cruise to Mexico. Once he arrives there, get one of our people to pay a reliable local mobster and have Parnell robbed and shot."

"I'll have an envelope mailed and sent to his house with a letter and two tickets tomorrow."

CHAPTER VI

Patrick, THE best problem/THE best assassin, assured himself that the Baricon would come for him. Patrick was unsure, however, as to whether the Baricon would retrieve him and let him live or retrieve him and kill him. There was a thin line between being affiliated with the Baricon and being a target. They operated under a strict code—as they were self-proclaimed humanity preservers and all. That was the very reason as to why they had hired the likes of Patrick in the first place. He was THE best. But, as of now, Patrick was THE best problem, also.

* * *

Patrick was being held in a special section of the Washington DC East Medical Center specially reserved for patients from the local jail. In front of room 540, where Patrick was being held, the police officers who were on the scene of Patrick's arrest were relieved of standing post by the city jailers who would be guarding his room for the rest of the night. Patrick's police pal's who had been discussing possible sentencing for him were gone. That, of course, made Patrick disappointed in a way because he wanted them to be there if and when his friends from the Baricon came.

It was seven in the evening, and the Baricon operatives had already received the order to have Patrick extradited from the country by midnight. The DIA was undercover in the hospital watching Patrick's hall, or "Robert Smith" as they knew him by the ID uncovered from his wallet. Armed jailers, undercover DIA, and Baricon operatives: it appeared to be an inevitable Mexican standoff.

Patrick was lying in his room staring at the ceiling. He was thinking of what the possible occurrences of the night might be. He knew that the DIA would be watching, and for good reason. He, of course, had killed three of their agents. He thought to himself that he should have known that lady dwarf was a grown woman by her enormously large head. How could he have been so stupid, he thought to himself acerbically. He gazed into the light still, wondering how the Baricon would go about retrieving him from the guardianship of the jailers standing outside his room. He again assured himself that they would come.

Meanwhile, the Baricon operatives were moving in on the hospital. The goal was quiet and discrete execution without gun-fire. Only darts would be implemented. If gun-fire was necessary though, a large assortment of firearms would be utilized. The Baricon operatives that were sent to execute this hospital extradition mission were fair-skinned British Muslim extremists from the UK and consisted of swordsmen, gunmen, martial artists, computer geeks, and explosive experts. They were disciplined and trained but had no knowledge of the scale or reason of the operation. They were trained, expert pawns. They knew that the disclosure of any information related to any of their activities would result in the instantaneous massacre of their families—no questions asked. They were loyal to the end.

They were all dressed in casual wear and entered the hospital from different entrances. They had pulled up a map of the building earlier and developed the Plans A, B, and C for the extradition that was about to take place. With a little luck, Plan B and C would not be implemented.

As the Baricon operatives were entering, the DIA was anticipating them to come for Patrick, or their "Mr. Smith." Their objective was to stop any attempts to get Mr. Smith out of the hospital and to detain anyone who attempted to rescue him. They also were undercover, and their presence or identity wasn't known even by the hospital staff.

The Baricon operatives came into the hospital like average, inconspicuous people who wanted to visit sick, loved ones. They came in caring flowers and balloons, the works. They came in with teddy bears and presents; inside the teddy bears and presents were highly powered explosives and a machine gun or two. Covered by the flower wraps surrounding the stems of the dandelions and roses were gas bombs, dart guns, and hand guns. The operatives walked into the hospital fully loaded, not expecting action, but plentifully prepared in case some federal agency was sniffing around (which constituted, again, the heavy artillery). There were seven operatives inside. Four other operatives were evenly scattered around the parking lot for the post-extradition stage of the operation. The seven operatives inside split up with two of them on the base floor, two on a quest to find the video surveillance room, and the remaining three in the hallways searching for Patrick's room.

They couldn't simply walk up to one of the front desks and ask a receptionist where their convict buddy, who they wanted to smuggle out, was. For some reason, that idea didn't sound like the wisest plan (there was just something about it that didn't seem right). So, they had to find him, searching room to room. Of the three looking for Patrick, there was one operative covering two floors. If they were lucky, they'd find him instantaneously, make the call to the four other operatives inside the hospital, and collectively move in.

The two operatives that were looking for the video surveillance room were at somewhat of a loss because the blueprint of the hospital did not indicate where the surveillance room was located. Needless to say, they had a plan for this, also. They had Bandcorp technician badges made. They approached a receptionist working at one of the first floor desks, walking like true repairmen, wearing their uniforms, and displaying their technician badges. The receptionist was a bit chubby, maybe pregnant, slightly over middle-age, with a brilliant smile and a name tag that read: "Hello, my name is Cindy!"

"Hello, how may I help you gentlemen?" she asked.

"Hi, my name is Dennis Styver, and this is my associate Alan Dandridge. We received a telephone call about an hour ago to come in and take a look at some of y'all's malfunctioning surveillance equipment," lied the taller operative with a convincing Southern accent. The accent had been practiced thoroughly to be convincing; everything had to be convincing. The outfits were bought at a thrift store and were blue—a matching, convincing pair of repairman's uniforms. The tool bags that they carried were convincing, the hats also. The whole ensemble looked innocent, while the whole ensemble contained enough artillery to wage an LA gang war.

Cindy had a look of confusion on her face; she didn't know where in the world the surveillance room was. Where in the devil was it, she thought.

"You know, I couldn't tell you that," she said, still smiling. "However, I think I know someone who can. Hold on one moment. Let me call one of the office clerks up here."

"All right," the operative who identified himself as Dennis Styver said as he peered off at one of the surveillance cameras filming him.

The receptionist peered really hard at this Mr. Dennis Styver for a moment. Picking up the desk phone she asked, "If you don't mind me asking, sir, where are you from?"

"Why, I'm from Mississippi, ma'am. Born and raised," Dennis Styver lied again, maintaining his false ascent.

"Oh, really? I figured that from your accent. It's pretty strong. What part are you from?" she asked interestedly.

"I'm from a little place you never heard of just south of Jackson. A lil' old hick town with a population of about 361," Dennis Styver proclaimed, reciting his third-round fib as he smiled as though downright proud of the place he said he came from.

"So, what moved you up to DC?" she asked as she held the desk phone to her ear.

"I always had a passion for fixin' things as a young boy, ya see. A guy that I used to fix a television set for in Mississippi called me one day up to Washington, said he knew of a job that was payin' good. So I up and skiddaddled out here, and been here ever since."

She smiled at Dennis Styver, and called a lady named Diane to the West Wing reception desk. She continued the conversation. "Is that right? One of my good friends here is from Mississippi. You two have the same accent. I'm from the South, also. Tennessee."

"Now, is that right?"

"Yep, Memphis, Tennessee, right up the corner from Mississippi. I actually lived on the state line," she proclaimed.

"Now, that's nice," he said, turning to his partner quickly to avoid any deeper of a conversation. He was a Southern imposter and needed to get out of the conversation about the South; he had never been south of Virginia. He sparked up a conversation with his associate talking about the latest update on surveillance equipment, pointing out how old the cameras were at the hospital. They gabbled about surveillance until the clerk Diane arrived to the reception desk.

"Hey, Diane," Cindy said friendly greeting who appeared be one of her close co-workers. "These gentlemen said they got called in earlier about something with the surveillance system. Is that right, Mr. Styver?"

"Yes, I don't know what the problem was exactly. We were leaving another location across town and Dispatch called us to come over here to take a look at your surveillance systems. It was something about a malfunction with the recording system," said Denise Styver as though not very eager to work, bummed out from a long day of repairing things, also as though he had a real Southern twang.

"Okay, I believe they keep all that surveillance stuff over near the North Wing by, um, Operations. That's right, isn't it, Cindy?"

"Sure?" answered Cindy with more the tone of a question.

"You don't even know where the bathrooms are here. Never mind," said Diane jovially.

"I don't know why you asked me in the first place."

"Me neither," she said as she diverted her attention back to the repairmen. "I think I know where it is. Would you like me to walk you to it?" she asked, starting to walk.

"I think we can find it. You said it's in Operations over on the North Wing, right? I think we can find it. Really. I don't want you to have to do more work than you already have to do," said Dennis Styver, walking ahead of Diane.

"Are you sure?" asked Diane concernedly.

"Yes, we'll find it. We know where to find ya'll in case we get lost," he said assuredly.

"All right," she said as she waved goodbye to Cindy and went off in the direction she came.

They were in the surveillance room in five minutes. It all happened very quickly. The man sitting in the surveillance room was darted, and all the recording tapes in surveillance were taken out. The mission was set to proceed forth.

Meanwhile, the two other operatives on the base floor were executing the preparatory measures in case the mission escaladed to Plan C. They walked over to one of the break rooms in the hospital. They did not demonstrate the same kindness that the other operatives had at the receptionist desk; they walked in with frowns and pulled out their dart guns. The four women nurses in the break room, who up until that moment were eating canned spaghetti and enjoying their break, were now sleeping on the tile floor with darts in their necks. The operatives locked the break room doors and unclothed the nurses. As the nurses happened to be petite females, their outfits did not quite fit to perfection on the taller, buffer operatives, but the uniforms were sufficient. The operatives were now in all green nurse scrubs, pistol-packed, and in search of a vacant stretcher. They found the stretcher near the entrance of the Intensive Care Unit across the hall from the break room; subsequently, they grabbed it and went on an elevator ride.

Once the call conformations were made from the operatives in the surveillance room and the break room, the "repairmen" moved in to join the covert search and extradition of Patrick with the other three operatives.

Five minutes after they started their search, one of the operatives beeped in. "Two jailers on the fifth floor. Meet me near the elevators on the East Wing." With this announcement, the five of the operatives were standing in front of the elevators in less than ninety seconds. As they were walking down the hall on the fifth floor towards the room, one of the operatives exchanged polite salutation with one of undercover DIA agents, who was not privy to the fact that he had just came face to face with a Baricon operative. The DIA agent didn't think much of the gentlemen walking down the hall with balloons, bears, and flowers. The Baricon operatives casually walked near room 540. As the Baricon operatives were walking down the hall, another undercover who had spotted them coming out of the elevator beeped in on his direct connect line to the agent the Baricon operatives had just passed. "Doesn't a group of five men walking down a hall carrying teddy bears and flowers seem sort of odd to you?"

Simultaneously, the covert Baricon operatives were standing in front of Room 540 silently shooting darts into jailers. The DIA officers sprinted towards the room, pointing there weapons as they yelled, "Freeze!" The Baricon's Plan B was now in effect. The five operatives jumped inside the room like true Hollywood martial art stunt men. The teddy bears were opened and the flowers unwrapped.

Several undercover DIA agents rushed up to the West Wing of the fifth floor once a call was made that the action had started. Realizing their lack of artillery, they called in back up. Hearing this, the Baricon operatives knew they had to move fast. Patrick was in a four point chain setup. They noticed that he had both his legs and arms chained to the bed. One of the operatives retreated from the gun fight to get Patrick out of his cuffs. The operative looked over near the door where he saw one of the sleeping jailers. He hastily ran over to the laying jailer and grabbed the keys from his waist. He then went to Patrick's bedside and proceeded to unlock Patrick from his bed. Then, he picked Patrick up over his shoulder. Patrick jumped down from the operative's shoulder and asked for a gun. The operative did not look at him, ignoring him.

Patrick then yelled, "Give me a gun!" The operative continued to ignore Patrick, staying near the bed as the other operatives were involved in the flying bullet confrontation.

The DIA agents were no match for the Baricon operatives (how's that for national security?). The standoff came to a quick end, with five agents lying dead in the hall, blood oozing on the ground. Thanks to Patrick, that added up to a nine DIA agents dead-and-counting list for the day.

"They're all down!" one of the operatives announced. There was a new predicament, and thus, a new plan. The gunfire had been used, converting the mission to Plan B. However, Plan C was now in effect because the operatives were forced to cause a loud scene, and some of the patients in the other rooms on the hall had probably called either 911 or security after the whole gun quarrel (the operatives theorized that this was highly likely). The operatives wearing the stolen nurse outfits were called in.

"Plan C is now in effect. Room 540," one of the operatives declared.

"We're on the way, coming down from the seventh. We will be there in a moment," the operative said as he tried to pull out a wedgy that had developed consequent of the tight nurse outfit. He pressed "5" on the elevator panel and moved the stretcher so that it was ready to roll out of the elevator. When they arrived on the fifth floor, the other operatives were already ready to go. They threw Patrick on the stretcher (obviously, he was not being handled as fragile cargo). After the five non-nurse-outfit-wearing operatives handed Patrick over, they split up. They were trained to be invisible, and so they vanished.

The two nurse-outfit-wearing operatives pushed Patrick past officers, security, nurses, doctors, visitors and receptionists on the first floor. They rolled him onto the parking lot and into a black Hummer. They left, disappearing like their fellow operatives had previously. The Hummer pulled off and drove for about fifteen minutes, making countless turns and hardly any stops. The Hummer then pulled over into a secluded ally where Patrick was transferred to a stretch limo.

"Well, you all spared no expense," Patrick said right before he was punched in the face, bringing him to yet another semiconscious state.

Patrick found himself riding in a limousine with two large, suited men as he slowly gaining a sense of awareness about an hour or so later. It felt like something Patrick had read before in a book. Was this the moment when they would off him? Was this the moment when one of the men took a plastic bag from the inside pocket of his jacket and the other guy grabbed him while they both suffocated him to death? Was this the moment were he was to feel the suffering he had bequeathed upon so many people many times passed? Was he taking in his last breaths? He breathed slowly feeling every bit of life that he had left within him. For the first time since Patrick's childhood, he was terrified. Many thoughts came to him at once, but these were unlike the ones he had before when he was involved in the police car chase/murder/kidnapping. All the faces of the people he had murdered in the past came to him, face after face in random order. He looked into the eyes of all of them and heard their voices greeting him to their residence: death.

The suited men in the limousine looked very serious, but not tense, not frazzled, not worried. They had a familiar calm sense about their faces. This indicated one thing to the terrified Patrick: they were professional assassins who were about to kill him—or perhaps that was the hospital medication talking. He looked at one of them and asked a question he really didn't expect a reply to. "Where are we going?"

The man looked at him but did not reply. So, there Patrick was, loosely wedged between two large, muted men. Then, more thoughts came to him. The limousine was probably sound-proof so no one would hear his hopeless hollers for help. The windows were probably bullet-proof so that it would be impossible for Patrick to bust his way through if he attempted a window exit. Also, the windows were probably over the legal tent level so that no one could possibly see Patrick die within the confines of the vehicle. However, he seriously doubted that any of their possible ideas concerning methods of murdering him would be something Patrick hadn't done or thought of before. He truly believed that his techniques were some of the most original and he was proud of his work, even now in the lion's den. If they were to kill him in a way that he had never killed before, or if they were to perform his murder with more precision than Patrick had on a similar killing, then Patrick would surely die in disappointed anguish. He also feared this, oddly enough.

He had to keep his eyes peeled not as the hunter this time, but as the prey. Today was a day in which he would be truly tested on how well he could anticipate the hunter and be the hunted, he thought to himself. He looked around and tried to find some feasible inkling as to what the Baricon's plan was with him, the limousine, and the two large men.

He did not know how long he had been riding, but after about an hour or two, he found himself being led into a small, private jet. He was still wedged between the two large men in suits.

"Where are we going?" he asked again, not really expecting a response. He got one this time, however. He was punched in the face. Again, for the third time of the day, he was out senseless.

CHAPTER VII

From a spectator's view, a person of ordinary intelligence would ask a couple of questions. One: What was the status of the progression and existence of the mechanical human engineering project in Iraq? And two: What was the connection between that project, Ambassador Dell's assassination, Parnell, Gordon, and Gordon's so-called idea for the preservation of humanity?

* * *

At the White House, Gordon was sitting up at the edge of his bed in the Presidential Bedroom. His wife was out for the evening giving a public works speech at a convention for a labor union. Gordon turned his head and looked over at the mirror across the room. He stared himself down, self-analyzing himself. He turned his entire body from facing the door to facing the mirror on the adjacent wall. He stared into his eyes as he tried to see into his own soul. He looked for a few seconds at the gray hairs that were developing on the top of his head, and then returned his focus back to his eyes and soul. He looked himself square-up, as if he was having a no-blink contest with the guy in the mirror. He looked more, and then glanced away into the carpet.

Gordon picked up his phone which was connected to a new line today, like it was everyday to keep the White House Internal Affairs Department, as well as paparazzi, from trying to track his conversations. He could beat surveillance or "big brother", and for this very reason the country was a tremendous threat to itself because of the president's ability to wiggle his way through the system undetectable and communicate without internal inspection's knowledge. The presidents of the past who had not beaten the system and were caught in their scandals were simply idiots, Gordon thought. Complete bimbos. Changing his mind, he hung up the phone and walked over to his computer, indecisive once again. His indecisiveness was becoming a theme, and this wasn't a very beneficial reoccurrence with all the important decisions to be made. His mind was going a million different directions. He could handle it, he reassured to his reflection in the mirror. He was, of course, the president, he reminded himself.

He walked over to his desk computer and decided to check for any new memos from his Baricon contacts. Each week, the brotherhood of the Baricon would put together a proverb, and Gordon had such a busy week that he hadn't had the opportunity to read his secret Baricon proverb memo. Usually, Gordon would have to read the proverb over twice or even thrice, because they did not make sense initially. Somehow or another, through time, or maybe even a reread, it would all become clear. The majority of the Baricon's weekly proverbs had proved very helpful throughout Gordon's career. He logged onto his secret e-mail, the one even his wife didn't know about, and checked the only e-mail in his inbox. He folded his hands behind his head and began reading.

According to the science of perspective, an outsider looking inside does not fully grasp the inside reality, or set of inside affairs, which that outsider is viewing. Therefore, for an outsider to draw a conclusion on a reality that is occurring on the inside would result in ultimate incompleteness.

If one is to desire a full grasp of a reality that is occurring on the inside, one must gain access to the inside to fully understand what is occurring. All other pieces to the puzzle that indicate what is occurring on the inside must be unveiled, because without all the pieces, speculation must be called upon to complete the puzzle. It is important to keep in mind that speculation can never actually indicate what has occurred truly because it is based on theory rather than reality.

The delicate balance that exists in reality is precisely controlled, unlike the balance that exists in theory, or imagination. In theory, anything is possible. In contrast, in reality, everything is not. It is possible to theorize about anything and everything. However, theories, because they cover such a vast space of possibilities, can not be said to be reality, and thus are not real. In reality, only reality is real. Thus, conclusions could not be drawn on what is occurring in the inside from an outsider's point of view.

In addition, open-mindedness is essential to understanding reality because reality is not a theory. A theory can be constructed in an individual's mind without the call to look at other perspectives. Reality concerns all perspectives. Accordingly, while an outsider may observe what happens on the inside, the outsider cannot fully understand nor manipulate the inside. In order, to understand reality and thus understand the past, present, and future of it, an outsider must see the situation from the insider's point of view.

Hence, in reality, the future can be foreseen...but only by one who obtains all perspectives.

Gordon tightened his lips and moved them over to the right, like a tight half-smirk. He removed his hands from behind his head, and put his hands flat on his desk so that his thumbs were barely touching. He tapped his fingers: pinky, to ring, to middle, to index, and repeated. Looking at his hands, he contemplated what the message was saying. "Wow, I guess I can be a soothsayer," he said as he leaned back in his chair, his hands still on the desk. From a different perspective, he attempted to look at his fingers. "What's the future?" he asked his hands and fingers. Ogling his fingers, he noticed his wedding ring. It was a simple gold band with brilliant detailed designs engraved. He thought of her.

Coincidentally, as he was thinking of his wife, she appeared at the door, exuberant to see her love, her husband, and, secretly, her liar. There she was, his marvel of joy and beacon of life. What she was and how he felt about her, however, never moved him to ever tell her the truth. Maybe, it was the whole leaving him or strangling him part. He looked at her; she was breathtaking even after a full day's work. He smiled at her, inadvertently making goo-goo eyes in awe of her beautiful splendor.

She was still smiling, forcing anyone to think this love would last forever. Their marriage was doing so well—how quickly the tsunami would hit the banks. Without the lies and deception on Gordon's part, they would probably be the perfect married couple. Upon her entrance, she forced her blazer buttons undone and threw the blazer off somewhere onto the wooden floor in the room. She kicked off her shoes, moped around in a directionless manner toward the bed, keeping her eyes on Gordon. She plopped on it belly first, smiling at him. "Wow, it has been such a long day," she playfully complained, her face buried in the top bed covers.

"Honey, you have no idea," Gordon said stretching and yawning.

"Who do you think had the longer day, me or you?" she asked in a jovial competitive way.

"Dear, of course I had the longer day. I'm the only man in the world who is blessed to have twenty-five hours in a day, eight days in a week, and three hundred and sixty-seven days in a year," he said as if he was really arguing, still yawning, still stretching, still smiling at her.

"Aw, poor baby, are you tired?" she asked as if in serious pity of his condition.

"Yes!" he exclaimed demanding affection. As he walked over to her, he asked, "Are you packed and ready for our little rendezvous to Switzerland this weekend for the World Dinner?"

She was still smiling as she rolled over to her back. "Yes, I'm looking forward to the World Dinner. It should be a nice little getaway. I hear the food is divine. The former First Lady was telling me all about the annual dinner at the Women in Government conference last week. You need to get some rest sometime this week for it—you've been looking so tired. How many meetings did you have today?"

"Too many, dear. I had a Cabinet meeting earlier that lasted over four hours. Then, I had a meeting with some of the guys from the CIA which lasted another three—it was madness encircling the house today. We're trying to figure out this whole dead ambassador situation in Iraq. We've been keeping it under wraps; however, I seriously doubt it will be able to stay clandestine for long."

"You say that so offhandedly. 'This whole dead ambassador situation.' It's a big deal, isn't it?"

"Yes, of course it's a very big deal. However, whenever you sit in a room talking about a particular matter for an infinite number of hours, it loses a bit of the sympathetic recognition when you mention it and obtains a more strategic-minded referral. The ambassador's name is Alan Dell, and his wife has been worrying our embassy in Iraq sick wanting to speak with him all day. She picked the perfect day to have some very important news in which she claims her husband must know."

"She doesn't know about his death, either?"

"No."

"It sounds like a bit of underhanded politics is stirring. Why does this Alan Dell death have to be swept under the rug?"

"Well, it's a long story. Some of the staff chiefs think we need to go covert in order to find the killer—or perhaps killers. Plus, it's supposed to be confidential."

"So," she sat up on the bed, "I'm not important enough to know about what is going on in the big, bad White House? I live here for heaven's sake! I can know everything I want. What do you have to say to that, Mr. President?"

"That's right."

"What's that?"

"I'm the president, babe. I make the rules," Gordon replied, now standing to his feet, beating his chess like the old, retired version of Tarzan.

"Oh, I see. I'm scared now!" Pamela exclaimed sarcastically. Gordon walked over to the bed and plopped himself next to her, belly first. The impact on the bed made Pamela slightly levitate for a moment. He began to wrestle with her. She yelled, "Stop!" and jumped off the bed, playfully running for refuge. "I'm going to call the Secret Service on you."

"Oh, no! Those are the men that work for me. I better run!"

"Yeah, you better!" she said grabbing a pillow from the sofa. She lunged it at Gordon as he rose from the bed."

"Oh, that will certainly cost you," he said grinning as he ran toward her, pillow in hand. She shrieked as he came full throttle toward her, releasing the pillow. It was a good throw, but Pamela wasn't a fluke of a pillow warrior. She ducked, successfully dodging the soaring, fluffy weapon. She quickly retrieved the cushion from the ground and launched it at Gordon, too quick for him to react. He fell to the ground as if he had been shot, stumbling, pretending to be reaching for something to help him hold his stance, then fell like the blow had been too potent for him to hold himself up. Down went the president. He rolled around slowly on the ground a few times acting as if he was seriously injured.

She walked over to him in a triumphant strut and said, "Who's the president now, sucker?" She then placed her foot over his chest, victorious.

"Still me," he said as he pulled her foot knocking her down beside him.

"Ouch! I think you broke it," she said in a puttering pout. "Owy, owy!" she exclaimed. "My bones are too old for that sort of treatment."

"That's right!" he exclaimed beating his chess while still on the ground, "See what happens when you mess with the president?"

When Gordon was with Pamela, everything seemed to be in place in the world. All of his problems, his worries, all, could be fixed by these sweet moments he had with her—how quickly the typhoon would hit. He gazed at her and their brief, yet eventful, evening seemed to pause. They were both engaging each other with their eyes. Then, she snapped out of it.

"Did you hear about that man everyone has been talking about? The one that killed those DIA agents earlier today?" she asked.

The president was enjoying the gazing but quickly snapped out of it several seconds after, realizing her blank stare. She would be concerned about this and nothing else until she knew exactly what he knew about it. He could tell from that oh-so-common look of concern on her face. If it was important enough to stop a romantic moment, it would be discussed before any romantic activity took place. He sat up to prepare for the conversation, thinking of how he could make it a sixty seconds or less discussion.

"Yes, I just saw coverage of it on of the news stations. I haven't talked to anyone about it because I've been overly occupied talking with some of the representatives from one of the labor unions," he said (really saying in his head, "I don't know, but, hey, let's move along.") She was still concerned.

"It's horrible isn't it—the whole thing. Three government agents are dead because of some crazed, deranged man. I believe they said his name was Robert Smith or something like that. He was caught by a police car camera shooting at these other men—I think I recall it was three of them. It was like the Alamo with this man and these federal agents shooting at each other. He reportedly killed all of them, kidnapped a lady who was in the truck that the agents were driving, and drove off. The police car that caught it on tape was down the street and arrived to the scene too late to catch the man who drove off.

"Yes, I think his name was Robert Smith," Gordon said. (What he really was saying in his mind was, "Okay, now resuming what we were starting.") She still wasn't finished.

"How horrible! I mean, there has to be more to the story than some cold-blooded murderer just randomly killing those DIA officers. Did they say anything about a drug bust or some kind of quarrel the man had with those agents?

"Dear, I know as much as you know about the matter. I'm sure the whole thing will be brought to me tomorrow, if not in a few moments. So, why don't we light a candle or two, turn on some Barry Wh— " She interrupted before he could finish.

"Are you not concerned about this? Those were federal agents," she said, playing with him now.

"Not now. Now, I'm concerned about you and I," he said flopping on to his back on the bed.

"Oh dear, honey, you've had a rough day. Do you need some tender love and care?" He nodded his head pitifully and they continued the gazing. The candles were lit; the Barry White was played; and then the lights went out.

* * *

Awaking at 7 a.m. with his beautiful wife asleep beside him, Gordon flipped on the television and saw it all on the news.

"*Alan Dell, an American ambassador in Iraq, was officially reported missing at four this morning. Alan Dell has not been seen in the past three days. For some reason it seems, officials have been trying to cover up the fact that he has been missing. Earlier we talked with several officials working in the embassy—they claimed that Alan Dell is still alive, but they refused to provide his whereabouts when questioned about it. However, we received leads from another source that suggested otherwise. It was suggested that the reason the embassy could not provide the location of Dell was because he is dead. For more coverage, please stay tuned as the story unfolds.*"

Immediately Gordon's phone rang. It was Vice President Lannigan. "You see the news on CNN?" Lannigan asked.

"Yes, I just finished watching it."

"Hey, we need to hire some of those press reporters to do work for us. We need to sign those boys and girls up for our intelligence department. Give em' a badge and a gun, and we'll know every international secret ever kept."

"The sad part is that's the truth," Gordon said looking beside him at his sleeping wife. She is so gorgeous in her sleep, he thought.

"Yeah, so we just hang tight on this?" asked Lannigan, making more of a declaration than posing an inquisition.

"Of course."

"Not worried?"

"Concerned."

"Think they'll get smart?"

"They're not that bright."

"Any other thoughts?"

"I'm going to let the news marinate a little."

"Don't be too lax, now."

"Never. Just cool."

"Macho?"

"That is you. How's vacation?"

"Last night was a ball."

"Mistress?"

"Now, I wouldn't be discrete if I told you that."

"She's still there?"

"Yes."

"Be careful. We have enough peril as it is. She still asleep?"

"Like a newborn. Last night was a blast, though. I'll tell you that much."

"I don't want details. I'll see a horror movie later."

"Funny. Well, unlike you, at least I'm not funny looking."

"Just funny smelling, right?"

"Only when I am within hundred feet of you too long. Hey, but really, did Intelligence brief you about that new invention?"

"What invention's that?"

"Deodorant."

"What's that? A second grade joke? Your second grade joke probably has the same educational level as your lady friend, huh?"

"*Touché*, on guard."

"You're in Argentina. Why are you speaking French?"

"Okay, *tu madre*."

"And same to you."

"Right."

"Not today. What's the status of the operation?"

"It turned out golden."

"Where?"

"He's a hundred miles near me."

"Where will they think to look?"

"Plenty of misleads were dropped. They'll want to look in the Philippines."

"Good. And I'll make sure the project is well funded."

"Great. Too bad we don't have any of those news reporters working for us."

"Thank God. How about our old, retired English buddy?"

"He'll get the letter today."

"Good. When will the job be done?"

"If he takes it—within the next forty-eight hours."

"Just a regular old disappearing act. Who will be next?"

"You will."

"Again, same to you. Talk to you later."

CHAPTER VIII

His name was Omar Madani. He was the president's first choice to fill the empty slot of the Central Intelligence Advisor in place of the unfortunately retired Robert Parnell. Secretly, Omar Madani was a member of the terrorist organization Al Shidad. Mr. Madani didn't know that the president knew; the president knew Mr. Madani didn't know; and the president's Cabinet and Security Council members didn't know what both the president and Mr. Madani knew they didn't know. Mr. Madani did know that the Baricon was the fatherhood organization of Al Shidad. The Baricon was the secret fatherhood organization to more than half the American proclaimed "terrorist organizations" in the Middle East. The purpose of these subsidiary organizations was simple; they served as mere distractions.

So, it was perfectly designed that Mr. Madani was working for the president in more ways than he knew. Gordon could openly get away with so much more that it would be absolutely ridiculous.

Originally from Saudi Arabia, Madani was medium height with a sizable gut, which kept him warm during his station in Russia during the wintertime. He kept his hair slick and his shoes shined (like most military officers). He was very articulate in the use of the English language—he had abandoned his native accent long ago.

Omar Madani graduated in the United States from West Point with supra cum laude honors. After graduation, he was appointed to the rank of Sergeant Major. Following ten years of military service, he was confirmed by the Senate to the rank of Second Lieutenant. After five years moving up in ranks and providing great help in, ironically, Desert Storm in the Middle East, Mr. Madani found himself in the position of Lieutenant Colonel. He also worked as an officer in the Central Intelligence Department of the Army in Transnational Affairs. Presently, he was being nominated to become the new Central Intelligence Advisor to the President.

Gordon walked into the joint Cabinet and Security Council meeting with Mr. Madani—ten minutes late, of course. Before belatedly walking into the meeting, Gordon advised Mr. Madani never to be late for a meeting. Punctuality was key in the White House, he explained.

As they were entering, the president made no attempts to introduce Mr. Madani. He left him near the door and walked over to his chair at the head of the conference table, which had a specially designed presidential cushion. When he sat down, got comfortable, and finally looked up, he noticed Madani across the room and said, "Cabinet and Council, this is Omar Madani. For the past two days we have been discussing who to nominate to fill the void of Intelligence Advisor Parnell. This is my first choice.

Mr. Madani, come over here and introduce yourself to the team."

Mr. Madani walked over towards the president, absorbing the looks of skepticism that were emitted from the crowd of Cabinet and Security Council members. He walked confidently though—the looks did not affect him; he had received much worse looks during his career in the Army (notably, by the grenade-throwing eleven year-olds in Desert Storm).

Mr. Madani was going to be Top Cheese under the command of the Top Nacho—together they would run the coming war—Gordon smiled inside at this notion. Mr. Madani knew about the planned terrorist attack upon the US that was set to occur in the next two days. Mr. Madani's nomination to this new position was just so convenient, he thought. This thought was shared with Mr. Madani and the president, who knew that in the state of emergency, Gordon could appoint (without Congress' approval) anyone he wanted. Gordon was actually ready to get the terrorist attacks over with. He was ready for the planes to hit.

Madani never smiled, and he certainly wasn't about to start today. Gruffly, he addressed the members of the Cabinet and Council.

"Hello, my name is Omar Madani," he started, "I'll make this short to save time. Approximately twenty-four hours ago, I was advised by President Wade that I was his first choice for nomination as the new Central Intelligence Advisor to the President in place of the retired Robert Parnell. It would be my honor to have the opportunity to serve in this position. Also, I assure all of you that I would work my hardest to achieve the objectives deemed necessary by this administration of Cabinet and Council members. I'm not going to waste any time; so, if you have any questions for me, I'd be more than happy to answer any you may have." There was gaping silence as all the members of the Cabinet and Council put on their most intimidating façades to this intruder of their sacred gathering. "Well, if there aren't any questions, let's get this barrel of bullets rolling." He knew it was a bad expression and that humor wasn't his strong point. He knew it, and told bad jokes anyway—it was a military thing.

The president knew that the Cabinet and Council would not go too easy on Madani. Most of the Cabinet and Council was relatively new themselves. However, as top position holders it was their nature to be uptight about things of this sort. Gordon played it off smoothly.

"I see the looks of doubt and cynicism on some of your faces. Now, I would like all of you to consider this—wipe those silly faces off." Gordon leaned back in his chair at the head of the table. He looked at the entire crowd sternly. One by one, he made them all come back to his reign of blind submission. This was his crowd that was to be sculpted; he would make these rookies of the White House into professionals (or rather flunkies for him). So far, he was doing quite the job. His goal was to be unquestionable, supreme, and infallible in the minds of his Cabinet and Council. They had to trust him.

The same thing was true with Congress, the American public, and the leaders around the world. It was imperative for his survival as the supreme ring leader of the most powerful country in the world. He had to be trusted to be the dictator, as to be dictator was indeed his plan. He had to be trusted for them to entrust him with America's twenty-five hundred nuclear warheads, which he completely intended on gaining full control of. His strut for power and respect had been working so far—he was up in the polls, minimal

Saturday Night Live skits were being made about his mistakes, and Forbes and World had been showing him front page, cartoon, and column love with supportive praise (which was unheard of for new presidents).

The Council and Cabinet seemed to ease up a bit as Gordon's brusque look went around the table and hit all the Cabinet and Council members. By the time the president finished his facial chest-beating upon the Cabinet and Council, the members that still had ounces of cynicism in them pretended they were completely okay with the whole thing. Gordon asked Mr. Madani to take the vacant seat across the table formally reserved for the retired Central Intelligence Advisor. Madani sat, and at that moment was unofficially inaugurated into the office of Central Intelligence Advisor.

Gordon started the meeting. "Okay, report on the last minutes from our previous meeting."

One of the Cabinet members stood. "Yes, we discussed possible nominations for the new intelligence advisor, the new bill on works projects for citizens with mental retardation, and increased government funding for homeland security."

The president thanked Mr. Johnson for his report and moved right on along. Mr. Madani was sitting stiffly in his chair, analyzing the members of the Cabinet and Council, the room, the nearest exit—it was a military thing.

"New business?" asked Gordon.

"Yes, sir," said Margaret Shillings, Secretary of Labor. "The Department of Labor has been working on a proposal concerning Social Security."

"Yes—" the president followed in perceived interest. Personally, it was not on the top of his mind. It would be discussed. If it was the "popular choice" it would be presented to Congress.

Everything was about image to Gordon. So, this proposal would be heard; and even if he agreed with it fully, he might shoot it down because of that oh so important public relations aspect of his job. The popular choices had to be made to dazzle the nation and sweep everyone in it (or most everyone in it) off their feet and into wild applause for the tremendous efforts made by him.

Mrs. Shillings continued, "We have been working on a proposal that would amend the way Social Security is dealt with in present day. This proposal would end the mandatory Social Security deduction from worker's checks, basically making it optional for Americans to be under the umbrella of Social Security."

Gordon agreed with the concept; however, it was entirely too dramatic. It would cause a big ruckus among the Democrats and Republicans in Congress, thus splitting his votes in more ways than just this issue. Gordon knew that with the present state of Social Security and the way it was declining, major reform would have to be made—now, however, was not the time. He had to shoot it down, unfortunately.

"I believe that topic would best be discussed at a later time in a subcommittee meeting," Gordon said, moving right along.

"But, Mr. President—" Mrs. Schillings started, then paused under Gordon's uncompromising glare. "Alright, when would be a good time to go over this proposal?" she asked.

"We can discuss that at a later time," Gordon said firmly, moving on along once again. Mrs. Schillings had it written all over her face that she wanted to say something, but she didn't. Gordon's rule over the Cabinet and Council was strong; at this particular point, it showed well. Plus, Gordon had to set an impression for the new, susceptible intelligence advisor.

"More new business?" Gordon asked. His eyebrows were up as if he was happily receptive to any of their possible proposals—

though it would be a mistake to assume that he was. It was all a part of tact and diplomacy. If he ever got around to writing his book, it would include advice that good leadership is being charismatically diplomatic but holding good ground. After the whole tactfully blowing off Mrs. Shillings' proposal thing, one of the Cabinet members stood.

"Mr. President, if it pleases the Cabinet, I would like to discuss our Iraqi ambassador situation."

"Everyone see the news this morning?" Gordon asked, as practically the entire Cabinet and Council nodded their heads. They were his Cabinet, and many of them weren't even in a field closely related to dealing with the ambassador cover-up situation. However, he figured that he should make his entire Cabinet and Council feel like family if he let them in on all the minuscule secrets that really, actually didn't matter. They would feel like they were significant. After his office term, some of them would probably go out writing books about bad ol' President Wade that screamed "scandal!" But that was alright by Mr. Wade seeing as much of what they were discussing was of so little importance to the big picture. The ambassador matter leaking out to the news was not a good thing, and the Cabinet knew it. They were expecting the proper misplaced blame and the appropriate butt-chewing to fall upon them; however, to their astonishment and surprise, he did not hand them all of their heads on a silver platter. Instead, he seemed okay with the whole situation.

"The question is now presented, ladies and gentlemen. How do we deal with this situation?" Blank faces were scattered all over the room after Gordon's question was laid on the table.

Poor Cabinet and Council...they didn't know what to do. At this point, the president was nice enough to provide proper guidance. After a few more moments passed with nothing being said, the president advised, "President Abe Lincoln wrote in one of his secret memoirs to the future presidents of this great nation that when we make big mistakes it is important to, and I quote, 'Deny, deny, deny.' And, today we will follow that advice. We will deny, deny, deny... we ever knew anything."

With that and a few more insignificant proposals, everyone was dismissed. Omar Madani was walking out last and for some reason or another thought he would be called back in by the president. He was not; Gordon knew Madani would not be sure where to go or whatnot, but he left Madani in the hall, not re-inviting him into the office. Gordon sat in his chair and looked around. *This is a really nice room*, he thought randomly. He waited a bit, until he knew that the hall in front of the Cabinet Room had probably been completely evacuated, other than the Secret Service agents standing around, of course.

He wanted to golf, but decided tonight would be better spent breaking the wonderful news about being associated with a terrorist organization to his wife. He stood up, placing his left hand's fingertips on the table. He ran his fingertips across the table as he walked towards the door. He grabbed the knob, opened the door, and made his grand exit from the Cabinet Room up toward his room where his wife might or might not be. He knew of all the meetings and benefits she had to do today. When he arrived to their bedroom, escorted by two Service men, he walked in, not escorted by the service men—he thanked God for this. He saw her sitting on one of the recliners in her burgundy, silk robe and said, "Don't you just love those guys?" as he pointed back at the closed doors where he left the Service agents behind.

She looked up at him, beaming that oh-so-brilliant smile, and said, "They are absolute darlings. How could you not love those gentlemen?"

Gordon smiled back saying, "Yes, I know, dear. But, they always seem to feel the urge to escort me up and down the halls of my own house."

"Aw dear, they only want to protect my honey. I told them the first day we arrived here that they had better take care of my husband."

"So, this annoyance is a product of you. Thanks dear," he said sarcastically, half-smiling.

"See, you are different from all the rest of the presidents of the past. You see, if the president was a Democrat he had to watch out for all the Republicans to stab him in the back. And if he was a Republican it was the same thing vice-versa. You're an Independent, you must watch your back," she said this, laughing towards the close of her analysis, twinkling her baby doll eyes.

He looked into those eyes and couldn't, with all the might that he could muster, even attempt to tell her the shocking truth. He walked over to her and kissed her neck. She shivered at this loving kiss of affection. It was filled with mass amounts of love. She loved him so much, he always knew the right time, the right place. "I adore you," he whispered into her ear.

"And I, you more," she said running her finger through his hair.

"No, I, you more," he said.

"How much do you adore me?" she asked.

"This much," he said stretching his arms out as wide as humanly possible.

"Well then, it is resolved. I definitely love you more because I adore you twice as much as that," she said as she moved her fingertips through her flowing hair once more. "World Dinner in four days," she reminded.

He looked at her. The thought of what would happen the night of the World Dinner went through his head and nearly ruined his mood (the kidnapping, the holding of hostages, the threats, the guns, the possible nuclear explosions and such—it really almost wrecked his mood). Looking into her eyes though, the mood came back very quickly. "Yes, it is."

"I can't wait to meet the new King and Queen of England."

"Yes, that should be nice. I hear that the Prime Minister should be there, also. Did you hear that the Minister's wife has nine children?"

"Are you serious?" she asked in surprise. "They are just running a little factory of babies over there in that castle of theirs."

"Good thing we're too old," Gordon said.

"Who are you calling old?"

"You are old, an old hag," Gordon grinned, looking deep into her eyes, adoring her beauty yet once again.

"You're older than I am."

"What? By a couple of months."

"You're the old hag," she said still smiling.

"Me, an old hag? I'm sorry but I did not know I had a gender change."

"You did not, I hope, but you're still an old hag."

"Now, how is that? Wait. Let me guess—'because you say so', right?"

"Right."

Gordon fake coughed loudly, pretending to almost gag. "Oh... oh, OK."

"Oh, dear, are you okay?"

"Yes, I'm fine. Just got something caught in my throat, I suppose."

She mocked him, "Oh... oh, OK."

"Oh... now you're a mocking old hag."

"Why would I mock you, when I'm me. *Paaahlease.*"

"Hey, it is okay to want to be like me. I'm just the singular most powerful man in the world."

"So...what's that supposed to mean?"

"It's okay. Monkey see, monkey do."

"So now I'm a monkey?"

"I didn't say that."

"So where did 'monkey see, monkey do' come from?"

"Nowhere."

"O...oh, OK." She mocked his coughing statement again.

"Are you feeling a bit of self-conviction? Or, are you reliving bad experiences as a child? Aww, did they call you a monkey as a child?"

"That's okay. You're just mad because you're not me, that's all."

"You're right. I'm just mad because I'm not you."

"I knew it the whole time."

"You did?"

"Yes, siree. It's okay. Keep watching; maybe you'll learn a little something."

"Oh, ok. I'm watching."

"Why is your hand creeping up my thigh?"

"Oh! I'm sorry. Was that my hand?"

"Yes, that was your hand," she said with wide eyes, moving her head slightly from side to side like a pig-tailed school girl.

"Oops, I'm so sorry, dear." He withdrew his left hand from her inner thigh, and moved his right hand onto the opposite inner thigh."

"Bad Boy!"

"What am I—your dog?"

"Down! Down! Sit!"

He was still looking deep into her eyes. He withdrew and said, "Fine. If you want to be mean, than that's alright." He walked over to the bed and laid down. "I'll do my latest trick. This is called 'playing dead.'"

"Dear, did I hurt your liwal' feelings?"

"Nope. I'm fine."

"Aww, I hurt your liwal' feelings."

"I'm playing dead; please don't disturb me."

"Oh. Shhhhh. I'll be quiet." She was still sitting in the recliner as he was lying motionless on the bed. A moment passed before she slowly and stealthily got up and walked over to the bed.

He looked up and saw her standing there, sexier now than she had ever been before. Her silk robe fell from her shoulders.

CHAPTER IX

Precisely 5,323 miles south of the White House, Patrick was being held in a small rural town in Middle of Nowhere, Argentina. And of course, he was being detained in a dark, scary cave under the supervision of the same brawny Baricon operatives from his limousine extradition. He awoke with a slight mental numbness. He had definitely been heavily drugged. He saw the two men, still in suits. He knew that he was in a cave from the hallow sound of the enclosed, empty ambiance. If he shouted there would probably be rumbling echoes triggering bats to scatter around and so on and so forth. He also heard the dripping of water that is so often associated with caves. The dripping sounded distant, but the sound was amplified because of the hollow interior of the cave, making it echo— or maybe it was the drugs making everything sound uncanny to him.

One of the burly suits said something and gave Patrick the headache of a lifetime. The drugs that were obviously in Patrick made it seem like the man was yelling vociferously in his ear. In reality, the beefy fellow was speaking in a medium tone, not in a whispering tone, but certainly nowhere near the yelling tone Patrick was hearing. Painfully affected by operative's vocal projection, Patrick couldn't help but squeeze his eyes tightly together as he felt the excruciating headache the operative had triggered. To Patrick, it felt as though a nuclear explosion had been set off in his head—the worst hangover he'd ever had. He was definitely just getting off of or on some drug.

"He's still feeling the effects of the serum," one of the suits said to the other. Patrick felt the horrible effects of this statement as well—it sounded like a deep toned siren was going off directly in front of his ears.

"Put him back to sleep?" Beefy Suit #1 asked Beefy Suit #2. Patrick was praying that they would just proceed to knock him out again, because the pain felt like something that had to have terminal effects. Put me back to sleep, Patrick hoped.

Beefy Suit #2 nodded and granted Patrick's silent wish. He was out cold once again. "How long will it be before he awakes?" asked Beefy Suit #2, the granter of Patrick's wish.

"Probably a few hours."

"Here. Give him some of this. The doctor said it should alleviate him if he showed symptoms of a mild migraine upon waking."

The beefy operative took the needle and syringed it into Patrick in the arm. The two walked over to the mouth of the cave and exited. The day was cloudy with the sun barely permeating the thick blanket of clouds. The air was moist and it appeared as if it would rain soon. In symbolic comparison, the day wasn't looking too bright for Patrick who had been drugged and knocked out numerous times in the past twenty-four hours.

"Are you getting a signal in here?" Beefy Suit #1 asked.

"Looks like we might have to take a ride a few miles south nearer to the city to get better reception."

"How about our detainee?"

"He'll be sleep for awhile. We will be back in about half of an hour."

"Let's pick up a quick meal on the way. I almost deep-fried one of the cave bats in here. The two brawny, suited operatives rode off into the sunset in search of a phone signal and food. Patrick, sadly, was not going out to lunch as he was lying on the ground in the cave, powerfully drugged.

As he was lying deep in a mental pool of hospital medications and sedative drugs, the combination of all the drugs seemed to provide an anomalous chemical reaction because Patrick surprisingly was waking up, still with an unbearable migraine. He cursed his agonizing consciousness. He rolled on the ground in pain, hands bound behind his back, tasting the delicious dirt his mouth had been inadvertently collecting on the ground. He felt like yelling; however, he knew that if he yelled his migraine would only get worse. For another reason, the energy that would have to be exerted would be entirely too exhausting. He held his tongue from yelling and made not a peep. He was still rolling on the ground, though trying to manage the pain, trying to cope (the rolling wasn't really helping, but why not roll around in pain a bit?).

Why can't I be cataleptic now, Patrick thought. *Who hired those guys? What idiots!* Patrick raved these thoughts in his head. Did his mental raving help? No. Did it make him feel better? Like anyone else: yes, internally moaning and complaining helped. At this moment, Patrick was no longer concerned about his fate, just merely ready to get out of the cave and onto death or whatever awaited him. The great assassin had had enough. Anything would be better than what he was going through, and he hoped for a savior to take him out of his wretched predicament. Perhaps, something of a divine intervention took place, because that savior was standing right in front of him. It was his *deus ex machine.*

"Hello, Patrick," a voice said to him. Patrick could understand the words, but the sound had a tremendously painful effect on him. "Do you like Patrick Rhodes or Robert Smith?" the voice asked.

Patrick didn't respond; he just hoped that whoever this was would stop talking and giving him the headache of the century.

"I'm the only one that can help you, Patrick Rhodes/Robert Smith," the voice said. Patrick wished the voice would stop before it killed him. "They got you messed up pretty bad, don't they?" Patrick rolled over to his face and just laid still, face on the dirt ground again. The voice continued, "All right, I'll save the talking for later." Patrick felt himself being lifted up; his arms suddenly became free with a click sound from the cuffs around his hands. Patrick was hauled over the back of, well, whoever this was.

Two hours later, Suit #1 and #2 returned to the cave to find that Patrick was gone. They searched around the cave and found traces of nothing. Where had Patrick gone? With no sign of Patrick (but with full bellies from their lunches), Suit # 1 and #2 rushed outside to see if they could spot the drugged detainee.

"He could not have gone far," Suit #1 said to Suit #2.

"He should not have gone anywhere."

"There! Wheel tracks on the path."

"Dammit!" They exclaimed in unison. They ran over to their Hummer and drove swiftly over to the tracks. Following the path, up about half a mile past the scattered trees and grass of the area of Middle of Nowhere, Argentina, the Beefy Suit #1 and 2 found themselves at somewhat of a loss. The tracks had ended, and an immobile Toyota was sitting in the middle of the pathway. The two operatives jumped out onto the dirt road in the middle of the forest and approached the vehicle. In it? No one. The two beefy operatives exchanges a few mutual colorful metaphors and indecencies, cursed some more, and ran back to the vehicle. It looked like Patrick had been extradited once again; though this time, the Baricon weren't the ones moving him.

* * *

Patrick awoke to the sweet aroma of heat and sweat. He tried to open his eyes, but failed on the first attempt. He tried to maybe rise, but failed at that also. He tried to regain some type of consciousness, but again was let down by disappointment. He could not move, he could not talk, perhaps he could use the restroom on himself if he really wanted to. However, at this particular time, he had no immediate desire to do so. There could be no halfway attempts at it if he decided to, because at his state of being any movement would take a great amount of mental effort, even if it was urination. Just for the sake of not giving up, Patrick tried to get himself up once again. This time was an even bigger bolt from the blue: He didn't move (surprise, surprise). He was bound to the bed, not by cuffs, not by ropes, but by himself. Paralyzed for the time, he was his only restraint.

Alan Dell was standing over him beside the bed, watching. He observed as Patrick's eyes ran rapid under his eyelids. He watched as it seemed as though Patrick was really trying to break himself out of his paralyzed vegetable state. It would only be temporary, Dell knew. He also knew that he could have given Patrick something to give Patrick back control of his limbs, but he didn't. The reason was not based on shear thrill of letting the poor, sedated assassin struggle for bodily movement. It was that when he finally was eased of the pain and paralyzed no more, he would be more receptive to what Dell was going to tell him. He would be more receptive because of his mental fatigue. Dell stood over him, wiping more sweat off of Patrick's head. It was a sad sight for anyone to see. Patrick was sweating so hard that he could actually drown himself and die (kind of like his commander in the Army died when Patrick tied him up and left him during that hot summer day in Cuba).

After about an hour, Patrick finally regained the ability to move his eyelids. He was not only able to feel but he could also very limitedly move a body part or two. He attempted to move a limb, any limb, but was unable to succeed in his endeavor. As he laid there with his eyes open, he saw a face. He fell asleep again.

He awoke an hour later. The face looked vaguely familiar to Patrick; it could have been the drugs, though. The face started talking to him. Patrick was happy to find that as the face talked it did not feel like someone was yelling a migraine into his brain. The voice still sounded a little irregular—probably the drugs.

"Hello, Patrick. How are you today?" the voice asked. Patrick answered the question in his head, but nothing came out of his mouth. Who was this standing over him, Patrick wondered. Dell looked at the unresponsive Patrick and added, "Still not all the way here."

"Where am..." Patrick struggled to get out, not able to finish the last part of the question.

"That's not important right now," replied Dell. Typically, Patrick would have walked out once given this type of ambiguous response, but he could hardly feel his feet, not to mention move them.

"Where..." he said again in a forceful whisper.

"Save your strength to ask questions for later. I need you to listen closely right now." Patrick closed his eyes in defiance to this command. Simultaneously, he felt a very strong shock spurt into his arm. He was yelling helplessly on the inside as the pain from this unknown object caused a very quick, but fervent, electrical twinge.

"Keep your eyes open, Patrick. It feels better." Again, Patrick closed his eyes out of defiance; he was never good with taking orders. But, as a consequence, in his defiance he once more felt the strong, this time stronger and longer, shock of whatever it was shocking him. He yelled out curse words of many different variations in his head this time. At this point, Patrick found himself in an indisposed state of submission under the control of the electric weapon being used against him.

Alan Dell, or "the face" according to Patrick, continued. "Like I said, I would like you to pay very close attention to what I am about to tell you. It is vital that you pay close attention to every detail. Alright, Patrick Rhodes/Robert Smith/whatever you want to be called today. This is the scenario. You are now in a location that I will not disclose to you for several reasons. One reason I'm not going to disclose your location to you is because you are a smart guy, and I wouldn't make the mistake of underestimating a skillful assassin such as yourself.

"Another reason is that I want you to understand the state of inability that you find yourself in. You don't know where you are, Patrick. I am in control. And until you fully submit to me and the tasks in which I would like for you to fulfill, you will continue to be helpless until your grave. Or perhaps, your spot at the bottom of the river. I'll make this simple for you since you are heavily drugged right now.

"Here's the deal—plain and simple. You do what I say, and you live. Don't do what I say, well, you find that spot I was just telling you about at the bottom of the river. So how about it, Patrick Rhodes/Robert Smith? What do you say?"

Patrick disputatively held onto his state of stubbornness.

He did not answer. Consequently, He once again felt the shock, and once again he was in a state of submission.

"Listen, Patrick, let's not make this harder than we have to. I'm not a ruthless killer and I don't really want to kill you. However, I will. And very quickly, I might add. You see, we have something in common. We have nothing to lose except our mortal goddamn lives, which isn't really that much. I had plans when I woke this morning. Those plans included using the restroom, eating breakfast, and gaining control of you. I know that might sound kind of strange, but in all frankness, that's the deal. You need to understand I'm not trying to make you into my slave or anything like that, but you will obey everything I say and be very damned happy doing it, or this whole thing's not going to work. Your life is in your hands. You are incapable of moving your hands, but you get what I'm saying. So, how about it, Patrick? Do you want to do it the easy way or the hard way?"

"What...would be the...easy one?" Patrick said as loud as he could which only came out as a murmur.

"The easy one would consist of you subjecting to my every wish and command, basically."

"Sounds like...a no," Patrick said upon feeling a sharp pain for the fourth time in the day, evening, night, or whatever time it was.

"Sounds like you are setting yourself up for a hurtin'."

"Who...do you work...for?"

"That's not an answer," Dell, the voice, said as he shocked Patrick again, this time longer than the others. Patrick was getting lit up like a Christmas tree during the holiday season."

"What do...you want from me?" Patrick asked slowly, showing through his voice his great pain.

"Not an answer," Dell said as he shocked him for the sixth time (he was keeping accurate count).

"Stop."

"Not an answer." Patrick was shocked again.

"Ahh!" Patrick softly exclaimed, again trying to use his loudest voice, and again failing to do so as he whispered.

"Not an answer," Dell said as he shocked him for the eighth time.

"Screw...you," Patrick managed to get out despite all the pain he was feeling throughout his aching body.

"Not an answer." Ninth shock.

"Who...do you...work...for?" Tenth shock.

"Redundant. Not an answer."

"Ahh."

"Not an answer."

"Ahh, Dammit!"

"You just don't get it, do you? Not an answer." There was a pause as Patrick closed his eyes as if dazing off. This little act of Patrick's did not work. He was shocked for the twelfth time.

"Trying to sleep on me will not be condoned. Not an answer." Thirteenth Shock.

"Okay."

"Okay what?"

"Okay."

"I'm listening."

"What...do you want?"

"Not an answer." Dell shocked him mercilessly again.

"Okay."

"I'm tired of hearing okay's; give me a statement."

"Yes," Patrick said painfully exhausted.

"Yes, what?"

"Whatever you want, asshole," Patrick said holding the "O" note in asshole as he was shocked again upon calling names. He was now coughing. There was then a moment of silence. Nothing was said; Patrick was getting himself ready for another electric shock.

"Okay. I need you to kill someone."

"Who?"

"This will be by far your most difficult assignment ever. And please trust me when I say this; I'm serious. You weren't taking me seriously a second ago, and as a result, you almost died. Let's take me more seriously from now on."

"Who?" Patrick asked still in a great deal of pain and agony, feeling the aftershocks of the electricity that had been freely flowing through his body.

"Your old boss."

"Who?"

"Please don't play games with me."

"Who do you work for?" Patrick asked for the third time. He was shocked for this.

"Redundant. Let's not go back to that. Let's progress, please."

"Who... do you want me to kill?" Patrick asked again as he gulped realizing he was being redundant once more. He was again shocked again for his reiteration. He was just a few shocks short of passing out.

"Redundant. Let's progress."

"What would...you like to know?"

"I already told you what I needed done. Now, tell me who I'm talking about."

"Kill Nahas? You'd have...to kill me first."

"Well, if it was indeed the terrorist leader Nahas that I wanted killed then I would have no trouble granting your little wish to die. However, that is not who I'm referring to. Your other boss."

"Wade?"

"Yes."

"You're...crazy."

"That's insulting." Patrick was shocked for the nineteenth time.

"I'll leave you here to think about it a little." Dell left the room leaving Patrick lying in pain. After exiting, he came back within seconds and shocked him again.

PART III

THE ATTACK

CHAPTER X

"We interrupt this program to give you a special news bulletin. Approximately ten minutes ago, an airplane crashed into the Statue of Liberty on Liberty Island in New York in what appears to be a terrorist attack against the United States. We take you now to New York, where Tim Carothers is standing by. Tim— "

"Thank you, Stacie. Exact details are not yet available. We have not yet obtained video footage of the plane crash; however, we are working to get a hold of footage soon. Today at 9:11 a.m., a commercial airplane plummeted from the sky into the Statue of Liberty. The number of deaths has not yet been reported but is estimated to be in the hundreds. We take you now to what remains of the Statue of Liberty."

* * *

It looked like something that could only exist in a nightmare. A shadow of fear hovered over the American population as they watched in trepidation as the visual of what once was the Statue of Liberty appeared on their television screens. Tears fell from the eyes of many; anger raged in the hearts of others; terror was felt in the souls of all.   Gordon was in a labor union conference when a service agent informed him that America was under attack. His reaction was well planned out and practiced. He asked that he be excused from the conference and walked over to his security personnel. He acted as if outraged when he approached them, gnashing his teeth behind his sealed lips. The Secret Service remained calm, as it was their job never to have any kind of human, emotional expression on their faces. They had to be like robots at all times, under any circumstance.

It was suggested that the president be moved out of Washington as soon as possible. The president went along, acting amazingly surprised and angered by the news of the attacks. He, of course, had no idea that there would be a terrorist attack. He already had his speech written out. Personally, he thought the speech was a beautiful piece of work. Definitely, it would be one of the top among the many presidential crisis speeches in history. He had practiced it out several times.

Vice President Lannigan was still in Buenos Aires when he received the memo via an e-mail forwarded to his business cellular. He figured he would have at least have gotten a phone call informing him that his country was under attack. No matter though, he figured. As he was thinking this, the inevitable phone call came in informing him that the country was under attack. He acted in astonished shock. He also acted as if outraged by this terrorist news. Now, he would have to leave his "strategically arranged" vacation and go back to work. He took one last sip of the pina colada, dropped a few hundreds on the bed, and left his Argentine mistress behind.

The First Lady was reading a book to students in a public school in Virginia when she received the news. She, on the other hand, was actually surprised by the news. She just could not believe terrorists had attacked America. A veil of fear immediately came over her as she wondered about the well-being of her husband. Would he be the next target in the attacks, she fretfully wondered.

Well, of course not, because her wonderful husband was behind the terrorist attack. All the Top Dogs were extradited from Washington quickly and swiftly as the next blow to America hit. This time it was Times Square. The American public was terrified and consumed by fear all at once. Within minutes of receiving the news, businesses closed, churches were found as the only refuge, and prayers were lifted. All eyes were on God and the flesh leader of the country, President Wade.

Did his conscience play with him throughout the course of the day? Barely. Did he lie to Pamela when he finally returned and met her at the White House later in the evening? Yes. America was now on its Ps and Qs—everyone was watching the skies. To most of America's joy the next day arrived without another attack. USA Today had still been delivered, and the country read the front page account that covered the occurrences of a day that would be forever remembered.

Terrorists unleashed a shocking air attack on America's most prized stock exchange center and freedom monument yesterday morning, usurping two aircrafts and then crashing them into the Statue of Liberty and the Times Square Studios in New York. There were no accurate approximations last night of how many people were killed in perhaps the most destructive terrorist action in American history. The number was without doubt in the thousands.

The horrendous occurrences of yesterday morning were the most devastating attacks on US soil since Pearl Harbor in 1941 and the terrorist attacks of 9/11 in 2001, and it created ineffaceable landscapes of destruction and chaos. One commercial airplane, which reportedly held over 100 passengers, ripped a blazing swath through the belly of the Statue of Liberty causing the monument to plummet to the ground, sinking the entire nation into an incomparable state of alarm. Then, minutes later, a private jet demolished the popularly known NASDAQ Building in Times Square and a substantial portion of the surrounding area.

The U.S. Navy, Army, Air Force, National Guard, and Marines based at home and abroad were placed on the highest state of alert, and a loose network of Navy warships and Air Force and Army aircrafts were sent out along both coasts for air and naval defense.

It has been reported that both of the hijacked aircrafts were loaded with the maximum amount of fuel, suggesting a well-financed and well-planned connive.

It is predicted that none of the 112 people aboard the two aircrafts survived. In the course of the rescue missions yesterday, the horrifying collapses of the Statue of Liberty and NASDAQ Building caused even more bloodshed. At least 200 New York firefighters and 125 police officers are presumed dead.

So far, no one has declared responsibility for the atrocious attacks, but federal authorities said they have leads that indicate the involvement of Islamic radicals with connections to fugitive terrorist Ichtiak Nahas, who has been associated with the 1996 bombings of two British embassies in Africa and several other attacks around the world.   In his post-attack address to the nation last night, President Gordon T. Wade denounced the attacks as a failed effort to cause fear in the United States, and pledged to track down those whom were responsible.

"America will not rest," he said, "until the terrorists who committed these cowardly acts and those who harbor them pay for their actions."

Wade promised that the American government would continue to run "without disruption," and federal offices and Congress are scheduled to be open today. However, yesterday was a day of extraordinary disruption—for the president, for the national economy, and for the country as a whole. President Wade has called for an emergency joint session of Congress that will convene today.

Wade was at a labor union conference in Washington DC yesterday morning when the attacks began and spent the day being transported from Naval bases to Air bases for security reasons, flying to bases in Tennessee, Arizona, and Colorado. At one point at a Navy base in Tennessee, the president rode around accompanied by a fleet of machinegun-toting soldiers in an armored Humvee. He later returned to the Capital in the evening.

First Lady Pamela Wade, Vice President Lannigan, the Joint Chiefs, and the President's Cabinet members were moved quickly to unrevealed locations in the morning, and some senators and representatives on Capitol Hill were temporarily moved to a secure facility 85 miles east of Washington. The Capitol, the White House, the State Department, the Supreme Court, and the Treasury Department were evacuated, along with the United Nations in New York and federal buildings around the nation.

The disaster started to unfurl at 9:11 a.m., when American Airways Flight 13, carrying 105 people from Newark to Chicago, crashed into the Statue of Liberty on Liberty Island, the landmark of American freedom and democracy.

Many remember in 2001, when militant Islamic extremists hijacked planes and crashed them into the Pentagon and the World Trade Centers, killing thousands. Yesterday's terrorist attacks in New York turned out to be much worse. Minutes after the first attack, a private jet carrying six people leaving Providence, Rhode Island for an unknown location, tore through Times Square into the NASDAQ Building with another devastating explosion. The collision shrouded New York's Midtown district in dark ash, and created mass mayhem. Workers, residents, and tourists were screaming, gasping to breathe, and running in search of a way out. Many died from the entrapment of flames, others instantaneously from the impact.

Among all the outrage and all the sorrow triggered by yesterday's attacks, there are uncertainties about lax security and insufficient intelligence, as Americans try to grasp how such a disaster could occur with no noticeable forewarning. According to federal officials, the hijackers who crashed the commercial airliner into the Statue of Liberty were armed with nothing but knives. Many ask how they were permitted on the plane with these weapons.

In recent years, counter-terrorism experts have discussed the possible threat of biological attacks and cyber-attacks. Security officials gave out warnings just a few weeks ago about terrorist leader Ichtiak Nahas' threats to America using these feared methods of attack.

However, yesterday's terrorist attacks caught an extensive security system, and an obviously deficient one, off guard. The military command center in the Cheyenne Mountains in Colorado, responsible for U.S. air defenses, received word just five minutes before the first aircraft struck the Statue of Liberty that an

American aircraft had been hijacked. The notification came too late for fighter jets to deploy into action, a senior Air Force official said.

Private buildings were also evacuated, from the Empire State Building in New York to the Sears Tower in Chicago along with the Gateway Arch in St. Louis.   America's borders with Canada and Mexico were closed, as well. This coming weekend's World Series Game 7 against the Yankees and Braves was postponed.

Wireless networks mishaps occurred under the bombardment of cell phone calls made after the attacks. The overwhelmed Internet search engines Yahoo and Google told Internet surfers to try television or radio for news instead. Couch and Grey Hound bus operations and Amtrak trains were also halted in the different parts of the country, mostly around major cities such as New York City, Washington DC, Chicago, and Los Angeles.

Last night, fires were still blazing among the ruins of the Statue of Liberty and NASDAQ Building, and immense amounts of extremely combustible jet fuel continued to hinder rescue teams that were probing through debris for survivors.

The National Emergency Management Agency dispatched eight search-and-rescue teams to New York. The Department of Health and Human Services sent medical groups and mortuary teams and initiated a national medical emergency cadre of 10,000 volunteers for the first time in history.

The Empire State Building went dark as a mark of national grief. In Washington, Democrats and Republicans presented a united obverse in condemnation of the attacks; after a news conference at the Capitol steps, members of the House and Senate delivered a spontaneous singing performance of "God Bless America."

"We are outraged by these terrorist attacks on the people of our country," one of the leaders of Congress said in a statement to the press. "Our sincere prayers go out to the victims and their relatives, and we stand strongly unified behind President Wade as our Commander-in-Chief in these trying times."

The shock of the attacks not only echoed in the United States but in every major capital around the globe. European, Asian, and South American airlines canceled all flights to the United States and called back or redirected those already on course to the United States. Flights over London, Paris, Beijing, Tokyo, Moscow and other capitals and major cities were re-routed over less populous locations. London's financial district was mostly evacuated. Safety measures were bolstered around the world at several embassies.

Panic trade in global exchange markets caused gold and oil prices to rise tremendously while stock investors in all major global markets dumped shares in the most frantic wave of selling since the stock market crash of Black Tuesday in 1929. In the Middle East, members of several religious extremist regimes approved of the attacks, but several of international leaders from the region gave their sympathies for the American victims and their families.

Israeli Prime Minister Salem Obero expressed disapproval of the attacks in sweltering terms, and described them as an "abrupt signal for change" in the global war against terrorism. Palestinian leader Ressay Tafara condemned the attacks also, though some Palestinians in Israeli-occupied territories and Lebanon rejoiced with happiness at the attacks.

The Federal Aviation Administration quickly cancelled takeoffs nationwide, diverted international flights to Canada, and ordered domestic flights to land at the nearest airport within minutes of the first attack before the second aircraft hit Times Square.

It all happened in a very short span of time. Shortly before 9:30 a.m., the great monument collapsed creating something of an earthquake, quaking from the island to the shores of the city. Smoke replaced copper and iron as the monument had abruptly imploded. Mayor Bill Randolph publicly advised New Yorkers to stay calm.

"If you're in the Midtown area of Manhattan or on Liberty Island, get out as soon as possible," he warned. It seemed clear last night that America's fight against terrorism will never be the same. The country's airports are supposed to revive at 12 p.m. today, but with top-notch security measures there will be no more offhanded check-in, and there will also be a likely usage of armed air marshals on most planes to secure the American skies from future hijacking attempts.

Numerous members of the Democratic and Republican parties affirmed that for all practical reasons, America is at war. At a conference last night at the White House, President Wade warned that those responsible for the terrorist attacks "should not rest easy."

For the time being, those enemies have not been identified. However, government authorities said they have strong indications from multiple resources linking the attacks to Ichtiak Nahas and his terrorist web, known as the Baricon.

Journalists with access to Nahas and his regime said that his followers have been bragging about preparations for major terrorist attacks against the United States in revenge for American support of Israel. Yesterday, government officials informed that they intercepted messages from Nahas' associates boasting about striking their targets.

Before the chaos in New York City, U.S. intelligence pointed to possible attacks overseas in Europe, the State Department warned travelers in a public advisory last Friday.

Terrorism experts have frequently warned that U.S. airport safety measures have been growing increasingly and tremendously permissive, backing these warnings up by multiple studies. When the Department of Transportation investigators attempted to breach security at ten airports a year ago, they succeeded 47 percent of the time.

"The security of airports is sad," said Terry Alderman, an Amherst University professor and terrorism advisor to several federal agencies. "It's not difficult to have someone get on a plane and inflict disaster." For the time being, at any rate, Congress will put disputes on health care, education, Social Security, abortion, and national budget issues on hold; possibly for the first time since September 11th, 2001, national security is at the highest priority on the dockets.

At the same time of the attacks, Rep. Gloria Butterick (R-Tn.) was getting ready to call for an increased military expenditure for counter-terrorism programs at a news conference. "This is a failure of U.S. intelligence, triggered by complacency and by a shortage in resources," she said. "Today, our government failed the American people." Nevertheless, that was a dissonant note yesterday in Washington, where "unity" was the catchphrase of the day. In his address last night, President Wade stressed the nation's unity, stating that "a blessed people have been offended to defend a blessed country together."

* * *

National emergency is defined as a state of national crisis; a situation demanding immediate and extraordinary national or federal action. The terrorist attacks that occurred yesterday were to be so tremendous that a probable state or emergency would be declared by Congress. In this case, according to the US Constitution, America would be under a constitutional dictatorship. This meant that Gordon would have the incontestable authority to seize property; organize and control the means of production; seize commodities; assign military forces abroad; institute martial law; seize and control all transportation and communication; regulate the operation of private enterprise; restrict travel; have control of the entirety of United States owned nuclear weapons and...control the lives of all American citizens. Gordon had it all planned out.

* * *

"Are you ready?" Gordon asked Lannigan with the USA Today resting in his lap.

"Good morning to you, too, Gordon. Everything seems to be going as planned."

"Seems so."

"Is the speech ready for your proposal in the joint session on Capitol Hill today?"

"It has been ready for weeks. I have a few kinks to work out with the specific details about the attacks and such."

"Good. Talk to you later."

CHAPTER XI

It was a tense morning in the White House. Gordon was calling in all his inspectors, intelligence directors, government agency leaders, and the Joint Chiefs. People were running frantic trying to set up all aspects of the press conference for the president's later evening announcements, political figures were swarming, and top officials were on phones receiving the latest intelligence information.

* * *

Pamela was still in bed, paralyzed by utter disbelief of yesterday's attacks. She was sitting up with the covers wrapped tightly around her as she watched the plane crashes repeatedly. They never seemed to get old to her. The news had a particular way of repeating single events over and over and over again, dramatizing the terrifying scenes to make them appear more theatrical each time—it was a news thing. The same terror existed every time on the television screen as she saw the plane hit the Statue of Liberty, then the other airplane hit Times Square. She watched as up-to-the-minute news broke constantly. The news anchors were continuously interviewing experts on terrorism, authors of books on military tactics, history professors from Ivy League universities, and other "specialists." CNN went to commercial and sure enough, there was more footage of the attacks on MSNBC News. A new angle this time; and it brought her to tears. She cried a lot throughout the morning. Would her husband be next? Was her aunt in New York safe? Did she know any other victims of the crashes? These types of questions were commonly wondered by many Americans as they all watched the plane crashes again and again on the news. It was one of the most emotional days in American history.

* * *

Gordon was not in bed when Pamela woke up in the morning. She stayed up late the night before watching the news and crying, asking questions, which even Gordon could not possibly answer, and calling relatives in New York. Her aunt was one of the people on the New York missing persons list. Last night, she talked to her mother for hours which put Gordon to sleep around midnight. She did not finally whimper herself to sleep until about 4 a.m. Gordon had awaken at six and began his day, first talking to Vice President Lannigan, and then having his morning coffee with two teaspoons of sugar, a smidgen of cream, and his favorite Arabian spice.

Two topics were primarily on his mind. The first was telling his wife about the whole thing, what he knew and when he knew it about the Baricon attacks. The second was blatantly lying to the American people again on national television. The first topic outweighed the latter. He figured he would use his charismatic charm and witty intellect on her. Then, he reminded himself that he was not trying to get her phone number in college. He changed his mind and figured he would use his sincere, from-the-heart approach.

He figured that there were three possible outcomes after he told her that he was behind the terrorist attacks in New York, planned to kidnap world leaders and their wives at the World Dinner, and make the leaders meet his every demand. The first possible outcome of divulging this to her was that she'd kill him. This outcome was not too far fetched, but he sincerely hoped that it was. The second possible outcome would be that she would leave him. This second possible outcome was almost certainly one of the most probable upshots. The third and final possible outcome was that she would understand and ultimately stick with him until the end! *Was living happily ever after just for fairy tales?* Gordon certainly hoped not. The third outcome was the most desired but perhaps more far fetched than the first outcome which ended with Gordon found by the Secret Service, lying in the bathroom, profusely bleeding with multiple stabs to his chest. Gordon flinched just from the thought. He then diverted his attention back to his coffee with two teaspoons of sugar, a smidgen of cream, and his favorite Arabian spice.

It was now ten o'clock in the morning, and the president was high-boarding on the tides of the White House. He called a meeting, and all of the top, high profile officials were awaiting the president who was (as usual) fashionably a few minutes late.

He walked in with a power strut. "You know what this means, don't you, ladies and gentlemen? This is war!" He started unloading on infuriated, militant jargon in which he felt was necessary at this juncture. There was a lot of "military tactic talk" which Gordon knew nothing really about, but he always made it sound good. (It worked for the former presidents, so why not for him?) Gordon always thought it was funny how a man who had never been in a single military camp, or better yet never shot a pistol in his entire life, could be the head of the greatest military in the world. Gordon never even had a real comparison to even contrast military tactic to. There was football which Gordon had a particular interest in watching, but never in playing. Gordon was more of what they called a "brain" in school rather than an athlete. So, all of his theory on military and war was based on movies and books.

"Mr. President," Joint Chief Simmons started.

"Yes," Gordon said already knowing what Joint Chief Simmons was about to inform him of.

"This morning, approximately two hours ago, one of our Navy ships confiscated a DVD found near the coast of eastern Saudi Arabia. The video was catapulted from an unknown location approximately one thousand or so meters from the location in which we found the vit."

"That's refreshing to know that our enemies have downgraded to using DVDs as weapons," Gordon said as the room grew less tense. Gordon was in control here; if he wanted the pressure on, it was on. If he wanted people to laugh, then they laughed quicker than a talk show audience laughed when the light-up sign read "LAUGH." These shmucks were his puppets.

Joint Chief Simmons continued. "The DVD was transmitted to us, and we received the footage contained on the video moments ago."

"Have you seen the video?" Gordon asked. He actually did not know the answer to this question, but whether the Joint Chief shmuck saw it or not really did not matter to him.

"I have seen part of it, Mr. President."

"Why just part?"

"The tape is about five minutes long. I had two minutes to view it before I had to arrive here."

"Who is it from?"

"We believe Ichtiak Nahas and his regime."

"Dammit," Gordon said as if outraged; he wasn't. He had the people sitting around him believing so, though. With the theatrical entrance, irrational riffraff, hooting and carrying on, he definitely had them convinced.

"Would you like to see the tape after the meeting, sir?"

"Yes. This meeting will be quick. People, this is what I want. We have to be tactful in this...this that we are about to do. We must do this tactically, surreptitiously, and practically. We need to consider all the angles involved with what we are getting into now. I want to know everything that is occurring in the Middle East. It is not just Nahas and his regime or simply Iraq. Nahas has secret terrorist cells all over the world, including here in the US, as all of you know. I want to know about every major money transaction that is being made over there. I want to know about every Middle Eastern military action taken. I want to know the location of all of the terrorist figures from that part of the world. If one of them moves, I want to know about it.

"If someone tries to leave the Middle East, I want to know. Watch all the major weapons transactions being made. Run some analysis on weapons already obtained in the Middle Eastern area. I want constant memos on all of this that I have mentioned. I want to know what is happening in the air, on the ground, and underwater. Check all Middle Eastern satellites. Anything irregular—I want to know. I'm talking about the slightest things, ladies and gentlemen. I want us listening to every possible conversation we can eavesdrop on.

"Have all of your lines secured. Hear that? These measures will be carried out as surreptitiously as possible. None of you are to do interviews on any television stations. I don't care what it's about. If a news channel or newspaper wants to talk to you about a research paper you wrote on military strategy in college, decline. Nothing.

None of that is to happen. If it does you will be under breach of agreement which you all have agreed to as of now."

Panning across the room, all of the officials were nodding. Gordon still was not finished, though. He had plenty of rambling to unload on them to keep them busy for the rest of the day.

"I need the Air Force in Middle Eastern airs. I want top class air, naval, and ground oppression. Make the cowards nervous as feasibly possible. I want our ships all up and down the coasts heavily armed, ready to fire on anything or anyone appearing to pose a threat.

"Practically, we are in a state of war, so if there are any transgressions made while our people are in the air, there should be no hesitation to retaliate. We will not, however, under any circumstance, be initial transgressors. We will not be on the offense. Not yet, at least. We will solely play the role of retaliators in this until we sort out specific details and obtain proof and solid evidence as to who is responsible for the attacks in New York.

"We do not touch anyone, yet. Not Nahas' men—we touch no one. We oppress the hell out of the bastards though, and we do this how, General Robertson?

"Excuse me, Mr. Pres—," Robertson said in slight perplexity, not knowing whether to say "surreptitiously," "tactfully," or "practically." He got a really stiff stare from Gordon and made a quick decision. "Surreptitiously, tactfully, and practically, sir."

"Exactly," Gordon said almost interrupting the answer to his question. "There are no second guesses on this. There will be no deliberation on this. Now is a time of decisiveness. Now is a time in which we must do what is necessary to protect the people of our country. We must suppress the threat. We must gain evidence. And we shall ensure that justice be served. We shall ensure justice for the families and friends of the victims of yesterday and for the very victims themselves. We shall not err in this. We must be very deliberate about these undertakings and very particular in these matters. And we shall do this how, Mr. Madani?

"Surreptitiously, tactfully, and practically," Madani answered quickly, not about to make the same mistake as his new colleague General Robertson.

"Also, General Robertson, do you remember the rumored Baghdad Projects that we were discussing last week?"

"Yes, sir."

"Do you have the longitudes and latitudes on the location of that fairy-tale land that former advisor Parnell was talking about?"

"Yes, sir."

"Take a few crafts around the area and see what we can get. Maybe we can see something that we had not seen before. I want some pictures on my desk by midnight."

"It will be done as soon as possible, Mr. President."

There was nothing there, and Gordon knew it. It would keep military personnel occupied with something, though. Gordon knew this.

"The rest of you, dismissed." His inspectors, intelligence supervisors, government agency directors, and the Joint Chiefs stood and exited uniformly, all except Joint Chief Simmons. "All right," Gordon said as he stood. "To the movie room to view this DVD."

They exited the room and instantaneously upon stepping outside the door, Gordon was surrounded by his handy dandy Secret Service agents. He walked; they walked. He could have jumped; they would have jumped. Gordon thought about jumping then remembered his role as the serious, outraged president who was ready as hell for war. They walked up to the movie room and Gordon found himself a seat in the middle of the seven row, ten column theater. The movie room was mostly used for entertainment, but no one was questioning the president's selection of the movie room as the place to watch the discovered Nahas DVD. He sat down and the Secret Service agents secured the room. The place looked like any other movie theater, just smaller. There were red curtains on both sides of the 15 by 10 feet wide-screen. The seats were cozy just like those of any commercial cinema. The only thing the president was missing now was popcorn. He would have asked for some with extra butter but concurrently remembered his role as the grim, fuming president ready to wage war on every terrorist organization in the Middle East.

"All right, let's see it," he said to Joint Chief Simmons.

"Role it," Joint Chief Simmons commanded of the Secret Service agent who had never operated the film machinery in his life. The agent did not say anything about his lack of ability to work the video player, however. He took the DVD, walked over to where the projector was, and fiddled around hastily trying to figure out how to play the video. After fifteen seconds of finding the "Open" button, finding the "Play" button, and turning on the projector, the video footage was projected onto the screen.

The video quality was very professional as if it were filmed in Hollywood. Were the Iraqi's into filmmaking now, Gordon wondered as he watched the beginning of the tape. The scene was in a hotel or living quarter of some sort, which would definitely be identified after the tape was viewed, given the several clues hanging and sitting around the room. The hotel room was practically all white with random Middle Eastern males with long beards sitting around in chairs around the television and bed. As the camera man walked towards the other room, you could see a kitchen. Nice hotel suite, Gordon thought to himself. Then, as the camera man entered into the kitchen, of what seemed to be a hotel suite, there appeared Mr.

Nahas himself. In the shot, he was surrounded by about eight men holding guns in plain view.

"Eww, scary. They have machine guns," Gordon mocked as he saw this, still acting infuriated. Nahas had the whole majestic look going on, with his all white getup and his long, thin, precisely shaved beard which dropped down to the middle of his chest. "That beard is longer than I remember it," Gordon mocked again, still acting mad, still adding the essential commentary.

The tape went on with Ichtiak Nahas looking extremely serious staring the camera down. Gordon would have probably been actually afraid if he had not known the guy so well, and also if they had not been such good friends.

Nahas began in almost unarticuable English. Gordon was almost laughing at this part because, funny enough to him, he knew Nahas could speak perfect English. He had been well-educated in the language when he attended school in America. Gordon found humor in how well Nahas was getting into the role.

"Good evening," Nahas started on the tape. "I am Ichtiak Nahas."

"I thought that was one of his posers," Gordon said sarcastically as the video continued. The DVD played on as Nahas spoke.

"This video is being taped on the eight day of November. Me and honorable regime of my men of country, the party of Baricon. You should receive this film after you beloved monument, Liberty Statue, has fall. After you finance place of stocks has fall, also. We will not hesitate to kill more Americans. I say this, not to be mistaken as threat. This is but a promise. I promise more Americans will die on the grounds of America and outside of you country. My men of country, the party Baricon, shall rise to bring to end the American influence on our country. America will no longer take resources, which, by right, are ours. America will no longer have control of our men of country's militia. We shall rise to stop America in the name of the great Allah."

The president interrupted the video and it was immediately paused as he said in a fuming tone, "Wow! Gentlemen, have we been letting the Mexican government ship mass amounts of narcotics over to Iraq, because this bastard must be smoking on something. Continue the tape." The tape was unpaused.

"Allah has spoke to us, his chosen followers. The great Allah has commanded us to bring stop to America spread of evil around globe. No more will America expand it's evil influence. In the eyes of our God most high, we will crumble the evil of America. No more will America oppress the poor of other country. No more will America oppress other sovereign nation. No more."

Gordon raised his hand in the air, and the tape was stopped. "No more should you do those narcotics. Chief Simmons, go get me a report on which new Middle Eastern locations Columbia and Venezuela have been trafficking their drugs to lately." Joint Chief Simmons knew that he was joking in anger, but he knew better than to question what the president was saying, even in this instant. He began to get up from his seat, when Gordon said, "Sit down. Play the tape. This is absolutely insane." Joint Chief Simmons sat down and the video continued.

There was a silence, and this is where Joint Chief Simmons chimed in. "This is the part that I stopped at."

Gordon frowned an "okay" at Simmons as they continued to watch the tape.

Nahas spoke more. "Within the next 72 hour, you nation will feel terror like never before. You shall witness mass death in you country as a consequence of the great Allah's command. Havoc will be unleashed on streets of you large cities and smaller cities alike. What I say now is a message for United States President Wade.

"What," Gordon said as if challenging the projection screen.

"The havoc to be unleashed on your country can be avoided."

"And how is that? By surrendering the United States over to you and the 'men of you country, the party of Baricon'?"

"If you make unlikely choice within forty-eight hours to surrender five of your nuclear weapons to the Iraqi government, we will not attack and wreak havoc in the United States. If these nuclear weapons are surrendered peacefully over to the hands of the men of my country, the party Baricon, we will not employ use of these weapons but use them as a deterrent from future oppression of our people from foreign lands. The choice is yours, President Wade."

The screen suddenly went black, and Gordon peered over to his right. "Well, he's right about one thing."

"What is that, Mr. President?" asked Joint Chief Simmons.

"The choice is mine."

"Mr. President, you might have been right about those narcotic shipments over to Iraq, because Ichtiak Nahas must be smoking something to make an outrageous request like this."

"That fact is evident."

"So, Mr. President..."

"Well, it looks like we have reached an ultimate verdict; we know who is responsible, but we are still going to keep our eyes pilled on other suspects."

"Yes, sir."

"Have a profile report put on my desk. I want to know everything there is to know about possible plans Mr. Nahas might have."

"Yes, sir. Right away, sir."

* * *

After leaving the movie room, Gordon walked up to the bedroom. His wife was still sitting up watching the news on CNN when he arrived. "Oh, Gordon," she said in tears when he entered. "This is so terrible!" News of the attacks was breaking Pamela's heart.

"It's okay," Gordon said. "Everything will be taken care of."

CHAPTER XII

Later that day, escorted by a fleet of FHP Cruisers (but he was only occupying one of them), Gordon was rolling high as he strolled up Capitol Hill to present his delicately designed resolution to the joint session of the Senate and House of Representatives. Gordon's entourage of vehicles poured into the special presidential section of the parking garage of Capitol Hill two by two. The area was secured, and then secured again, affirmed again, and finally the president's door was opened.

He ascended from the Cruiser and had the immediate impulse to do his cup-handed wave, like he usually did when getting out of the Cruiser, but quickly realized the absence of the media in the secured parking garage. This was not a press day; this was a day when he would gain full dictatorship over the United States and.the pesky media, which was included in the full-control-of-the-US package along with the nuclear weapons and a variety of other perks.

He arose from the Cruiser and was quickly surrounded by Secret Service agents. He did his favor walk, and when he moved, everyone moved. He was pumping himself up mentally as the inspirational rhythmic beat of the song "We Will Rock You" played in his head. He was certainly on the verge of rocking the world.

He arrived on the floor in the joint session, and upon his arrival, a loud applause commenced. He was frowning, still playing the mad ol' president role. The frown was a sign of reassurance for all who doubted. He had to frown for these people to keep their faith in him for full revenge upon the terrorists. His mean face read "business." Surely, he was here for business; he just had a different motive than everyone else in the Senate and the House had in mind.

Vice President Lannigan, who served as the chairman over the joint session, pounded his gavel and officially began the session. The Pledge of Allegiance commenced. Everyone stood and recited the American pledge with a little more *umph* than usual. It was an exceptionally emotional day, and it was shown on all the faces of the members of Congress. Thank God they had a good president, they thought. *Thank God.*

"Good afternoon," Vice President Lannigan announced. "Today we shall not spare any time. Are there any speeches, motions, or comments?" Gordon stood, and everyone stopped to look at their brave savior. As they had routinely planned it out, Lannigan called upon the president.

This order of procedure in which was taking place on Capitol Hill on this particular day was highly unusual for a president presenting a resolution in Congress. Normally, a president would have already been on the docket and asked to come up to make a speech. Gordon was not the conventional president, by far. He sat in a seat on the floor where the Senate sat. He did not enter into the building from some mysterious backdoor somewhere at the time directly before his speech and leave directly after. It was part of his I'm-on-you-all's-team strategy. It worked; and most members of Congress loved him, or at least liked him, for it.

Gordon's relationship with Congress members was very different from his relationship with his staff and Cabinet at the White House, because his Cabinet worked in subconscious fear of losing their jobs. Plus, he really didn't need his Cabinet's vote to support any of his ideas. His Cabinet still liked him, but he wasn't quite as blunt and bossy with Congress as he was with his Cabinet and White House staff. He knew his crowds. These representatives in Congress and the constituents whom they represented were the ones feeling out the majority of the ballads. These ladies and gentlemen of the Senate and House were makers and breakers of his term, especially on this day.

Upon being called upon, Gordon requested to present his proposed resolution. His wish was granted, and he approached the center podium. He walked with great poise over to the podium with the confident strut which screamed "I have the sum of your worries under control." His proposed resolution was concurrently being perused by members of the Senate and House as Gordon drew closer to the center podium. Consisting of the mandatory legal lingo and legislative mumbo-jumbo, his carefully schemed resolution read:

Whereas it has been stated in an assortment of laws and other documents that the United States of America has the entitlement to use military action upon nations or regional regimes that have not formally declared war, establishing what has been called the `doctrine of preemption';

Whereas the doctrine of preemption calls for an extreme divergence from the regulatory peace-keeping stance of the United Nations;

Whereas not implementing the doctrine of preemption endangers the domestic safety of the United States as it creates a vulnerable model that may then be referred to by other countries, including other nuclear superpowers, as a failure to secure our country's own self-defense;

Whereas the doctrine of preemption examines waging war against a nation in which posses a threat of attack to the United States, and furthermore observes the generally accepted understanding, established in the Charter of the United Nations and other international agreements, that sovereign countries have the entitlement of self-protection, and that such self-protection may consist of undertaking armed, military action to avert a possible strike by an opposing militia;

Whereas policies of the United States have long had high regard and acceptance of the importance of the international treaties and laws in which we are a signatory;

Whereas the doctrine of preemption conflicts with the intent of the Charter of the United Nations to which the United States is a signatory, which declares in Article 2, Section 4 of the Charter that, `All members shall refrain in their international relations from the threat or use of force against the territorial integrity or political independence of any state, or in any other manner inconsistent with the purposes of the United Nations';

Whereas the Charter of the United Nations, while prohibiting precautionary war does not disqualify military actions of self-defense, reading in part from Article 51 of that Charter which states `Nothing in the present Charter shall impair the inherent right of individual or collective self-defense if an armed attack occurs against a Member of the United Nations, until the Security Council has taken the measures necessary to maintain international peace and security'; and

Whereas under the United States Constitution, the President, as Commander in Chief of the United States Armed Forces, possesses the authority to use armed, military force to defend the United States against an attack or possible attacks: Now, for these reasons, be it

Resolved, That--

(1) it is the opinion of both the House of Representatives and the Senate that the United States maintains the intrinsic entitlement to defend itself against possible or actual militant strike, as acknowledged in the Charter of the United Nations;

(2) the Senate and House of Representatives urges the utilization of the doctrine of preemption, because if it is not implemented the results would allow for a threat to the United States' national security interests; and

(3) the Senate and House of Representatives recognize that there has been a state of emergency and state of war since the attacks upon New York City on the ninth day of November.

* * *

Gordon began his speech. "Mr. Chairman, members of the Senate. In 1941, after the Japanese attack of Pearl Harbor, President Roosevelt said the historically famed words 'Today is a day that will live in infamy.' Yesterday, America was attacked. November 9th will also be a day that lives in ill repute.

"However, let us note one thing for certain. The weapons in which the terrorists used yesterday were not airplanes. Make no mistake in interpreting what terrorist attacked us with. The weapons that the terrorists used against the US were the weapons of terror. America should not, and shall not, stand for this without military retaliation."

With Gordon's renowned persuasive, political gobbledygook, he went on babbling about his plan for this and his plan for that concerning why America should retaliate on its transgressors.

He discussed the imperativeness of war and sending a message to the terrorist regimes in the Middle East. He paraphrased practically every word of his resolution, saying that the safekeeping of America was reason enough to implement the doctrine of preemption. He reiterated key points, as was a must. He talked of the cons of war, but demonstrated how the pros preponderated the cons by a long shot. He used the art of the emotional appeal, as usual.

He concluded, "We will raid every hole, bunker, cave, or wherever else the terrorists chose to hide in the Middle East, to find our attackers. We will use every resource we have at our disposal. We will fight until justice has been realized. Thank you."

At the conclusion of his speech, nearly every member of the Senate and the House in the building was on their feet, applauding wildly (well, as wildly as can be expected from senators and representatives). The resolution was passed, and it was now confirmed. A state of emergency had been declared—not really that significant to Gordon. But also, a state of emergency had been declared, AND thus Gordon was now the "Constitutional Dictator" of the United States—very significant to Gordon. He had the power. America's future, not to mention the future of the world, was practically in his happy palms.

* * *

Before entering their bedroom in the White House, Gordon sighed an "*alia iacta est.*" He found that his wife had not moved much all day. She was in the bedroom watching the news. This could not be healthy, he concluded as he closed the bedroom door behind him. "What's wrong, dear?" he asked, showing his deep concern. There was no immediate response, and really, one was not expected. Pamela was in shock. Good thing she did not know her husband was behind the attacks. He still was trying to get around to telling her—

something just seemed to catch him every time he attempted.

"What's wrong?" he asked again.

"It's just so horrible."

"I know, dear. We passed the state of emergency and war resolution in the joint session today. Everything is going as planned. I just need to get the United Nations to pass our war resolution now, which should not be too difficult given the circumstances."

"That's wonderful, honey," she said trying her hardest to flash a full, fake smile. She fell short in her attempt, as she only could form a half-smile, no teeth.

"Dear, you need to get out of this bedroom today. Let's go out or something. You have been in here too long."

"I'm fine. Really. However, I do not feel like going anywhere."

"That's very evident. You have shown that through your self-imprisonment in our bedroom. Come on let's go somewhere."

"They are still finding bodies. This is unbelievable."

Curse MSNBC and CNN, thought Gordon, continuing in his pursuit to get her up. "Let's go see a movie."

"See a movie?" she repeated with an emphasis on "movie." "See a movie?" she asked in disbelief of what he suggested.

"Yes, dear. See a movie. Look, I do not care what we do in particular. What is important is getting out of this room. This is precisely what our enemy desires," said Gordon. He sure had his nerve to talk about terrorists.

"I don't want to."

"Sure you do, dear."

"Like I said before, dear, I just don't feel like it. Not yet, at least."

All right. Like I said, I know. Though, sitting here watching the same news breaks over and over is not helping you. You want up-to-date news breaks? I will call in the Joint Chiefs and have them brief you on everything in the Situation Room. I don't care really what it takes. How about a walk down the hall?"

She declined once more, "No thank you. Really."

"Really. Let's just take a walk down the hall."

"I'm fine."

"That is true," he said working his head down the crease of her back toward her neck.

"Dear," she smiled.

"Now, that's what I'm talking about. A real smile. I miss that smile. Can I get another?"

She quickly displayed a very brief half-smile.

"Come on. Do I have to pay for a smile? How much?"

"A million dollars."

"That's easy. Congress just gave me $40 billion today. You want a slice of the pie, dear?"

"Isn't that money to help the poor victims' families and the war effort in the Middle East?"

"Yes, but anything for you, beautiful," he said with a smile. She smiled again.

"But you will go to jail," she said, puttering her lips. She was still very distressed about the events of November 9th, but she was trying to feel better. She saw how it was affecting her husband. Gordon knew at this moment that she was attempting to be strong; however, her feministic, innate sense of empathy caused her so much pain as she had heard of such horrible things concerning the terrorist attacks on the news. She saw the bodies being carried out from under the debris; she watched New York pedestrians in tears from the destruction; she watched as they played the footage of the airplanes colliding into Times Square and the Statue of Liberty.

"They will be brought to justice, dear. I promise."

With this said, a single tear drop fell from her eyes. She put her head down and glanced off onto the covers of the bed.

"I promise," he repeated.

"You know, I have been sitting in here watching as new information is released every minute. I know I could get the more up-to-the-minute reports on the discoveries and all, but I am seeing what the rest of the world is seeing. And, dear, I am terrified." She wiped her eye and continued. "I know that's the trick of the enemy; all they want is for us to be afraid, terrified; though, I can't help it. Because...I keep wondering it you will be the next target. I keep wondering when they will come after you. I keep hoping that this is not the last time I will see you.

"And, I want to get up. I want to go speak to people and help in the effort to bring them hope. But how can I speak and try to bring them hope if I'm terrified myself? How can I do that when I, myself, am a target? And even more, my husband, the man I love, is. I can't—" There seemed as if there was something that she was intending to say following the *I can't* statement, but she kind of made it a complete sentence and fell silent.

Gordon reached over onto the bed where she was sitting and embraced her. If there was a moment in her life when she needed to be held the most, this was it. She was frightened for her safety, her husband's, and the safety of the country.

"Nothing is going to happen," Gordon confidently reassured. "Nothing's going to happen."

"I love you."

"I love you more."

"Please don't let anything happen."

"I promise."

"I don't know what I would do."

"Nothing will happen."

"I love you so much!"

"There's nothing to worry about. The White House is on high alert. Everything is being watched out for."

"Promise me you will never leave me."

"I promise." They embraced each other tighter for a few more moments. The thought came to Gordon that maybe now he should tell his wife about his involvement with the Baricon and share with her the fact that he was involved with the terrorist attacks. And even more so, tell her that, frankly, there was really nothing to worry about because since he was behind the terrorist attacks, they were not a target of the "terrorist regime." He wanted to (not really), but didn't. Therefore, instead, he did what he normally did—he changed the subject.

"Two days until the World Dinner."

"Are you still considering going to that?'

"Of course. It is important that we do not let the terrorists intimidate us, but you don't have to go if you don't wish to attend."

"I'll never leave your side."

"I love you."

"I love you more."

"No, I love you more." With exchange of the amorous devotions made, Gordon rose, walked over to the door, and closed it.

CHAPTER XIII

Two days after the terrorist attacks and a day after getting his resolution passed through Congress, Gordon was sitting in the General Assembly of the United Nations in New York. On the floor, there was a delegate from Argentina making a speech regarding something to the tune of preventing global money laundering or something of that sort. Gordon was not paying the speech much attention, seeing as to the fact that most of the leaders in the room had illicit funds in progress of being transferred at that very moment.

The political game that existed in the United States was universal even in the United Nations. Corruption in democracy was to always be present—it was stipulated by the Greeks and Romans in democracy's creation. Leaders of democracy were but kings of the people, elected by the people. Leaders from all over the world deliberated intensely on moral values and passed money under the table to get their way. Sadly enough, Gordon was often a part of this malpractice in the United Nations.

Gordon was going over his speech in his head before he went on to present his UN resolution. The resolution had been passed almost unanimously in the subcommittee deliberation hours before. This occurred partially because all of the delegates in the subcommittee deliberations had coincidentally received checks from an unknown source in Italy the day before the voting procedure. Some delegates in Subcommittee had the moral stubbornness to decline the bribe, but why not? The resolution only asked that the member states of the United Nations abandon the UN Charter that held peace between nations in order to help the United States with its own internal problems. The resolution that Gordon presented had activating clauses which:

A. *Encouraged* all member states to recognize the sovereign rights of the United States to exercise military force in time of emergency,

B. *Requested* that member states assist the United States in its endeavor to alleviate the Middle Eastern region and the world from terrorist organizations, namely the Baricon,

C. *Expressed* hope that member states understand that military force is necessary to bring a halt to the staggering effects of terror and the countries that harbor terrorist groups.

With these clauses, it was Gordon's hope that the United Nations in the General Assembly would pass his resolution. It would make his countrymen in America feel much better if the rest of the world was behind the great United States and its military. To Gordon, in all actuality, the United Nations did not matter. It was a mere organization started and basically ran by the United States.

The UN had a budget of approximately $2 billion a year. The United States used more money per month giving grants to undergrad college students than the UN used annually. Gordon had received a disposable income in the Senate the day before of $40 billion for war; therefore, in all practicality, the UN was somewhat of a joke. It was something to play around with so that the American public would feel "peaceful" with the world.

* * *

The UN was similar to a hefty lady window shopping, looking at a nicely dressed mannequin with a thin waistline. Imagine that the hefty lady had a size 17 waistline and she thought to herself, "Wow! That looks nice. I think I will buy that exact outfit." Well, first, the stores do not usually put up for sale clothes off the mannequin's back to merely convenience a customer. Second, the lady would not fit into the clothes, anyway. The UN was comparable to this hefty lady example in that human's are human, and just can't fit into the mannequin's outfit of absolute peace. Peace has always been a natural human desire; however, man has always been plagued with fault. Therefore, humanly it has always been improbable that long terms of peace could be completely sustained around the world. And like the store would not just sell their mannequin s' clothes, countries would not just sell their peace. All of humanity, like the hefty lady, would not necessarily fit. The UN pretended though, and many things came out of the UN such as natural disaster funds and things of the sort which were beneficial. However, as America was proving this evening, the UN Peace Charter could easily be overturned by that little clause in the Charter that respected all member nations' sovereign rights—meaning the United Nations respected the sovereign rights of every country to go to war.

* * *

Argentina's resolution was passed. Yay! The end of monetary corruption in government was now realized around the world—well, according to the passing of this resolution, at least. What a joke, Gordon thought as he approached yet another podium to present another resolution. Gordon frowned at all the delegates. He was playing his deeply disturbed bit again, which was really believable in a way. He had the sick-to-his-stomach expression, as if the occurrences of the past few days had absolutely made him want to vomit. It was another one of his delicately and intricately designed political persuasive tactics to making others feel sympathy for him, his country, and the horrible things they had endured consequent of the terrorist attacks.

"Good Afternoon, members of the General Assembly. It is far too seldom that I get the chance, so I am profoundly honored to be here today before an assembly over three quarters of a century in the making. We and our forefathers have been allied in this delicate union for peace for a long time. Delegates of the Assembly, before I begin my speech, I would like to thank each and every one of you for helping to secure the future of world peace.

"Our mission here in the United Nations, is to unify the world and see that the livelihood of humankind continues. Our presence is to serve as a united group that is renowned for safeguarding humanity and our common interests in survival. But, let us take a look at the word 'survival.' Survival is the act of continuing to live or exist despite. I say again for emphasis sake, the act of continuing to live or exist despite.

"The question is what are we living despite of? It is our human nature to desire to survive, and we wish as united nations, as human beings, to live despite of all obstacles that may try to prevent us from doing so. As humans it is our destiny to survive; however, we cannot simply declare survival and hope that it be so.

"An obstacle that we face today concerning our survival is the threat of terror. Several terrorist regimes throughout the world threaten our livelihood and for reasons that most, and certainly I, cannot understand. Many of these terrorist regimes simply wish the annihilation of the human race. These terrorist regimes bomb us without fair proclamation of war. They kill innocent civilians without a conscience. They kill our children when they have done nothing wrong. They kill our spouses just out of the sick satisfaction of witnessing death and destruction.

"There is a group of people that does not want to see us live on. They call themselves religious radicals here for a religious cause. But, I pose an inquiry: When has death and destruction been a religious cause? When has murdering innocent people been a religious cause? The answer is that these wicked actions are not of a religious cause, but actions of a great evil. We are witnessing a great evil in action in these strange and bizarre days when terrorists usurp aircrafts and destroy the lives of innocent people without any reason other than hatred.

"I need not remind all of you that we are here to secure the survival of humanity and preserve peace around the world. There has arisen a threat to the survival of humanity. My country and several others have received shocking evidence of weapons of mass destruction in regions of the world that are notorious for harboring this evil we call 'terror.' It has been discovered that these regions are also working to develop new types of evil in the form of mechanically engineered humans, as bizarre as it may sound. These kinds of threats should not be tolerated. We, as a body that promotes peace, cannot just sit by as terrorists, for the mere sake of evil, try to destroy everything we hold dear.

"We have a responsibility. We have a responsibility to ourselves, our people...our children, to stand against evil and uphold the delegate preservation of freedom and peace. These terrorist regimes that have sprung up in the sole name of destruction are attempting to jeopardize our natural born rights to be free. These wicked regimes are trying to taint our societies with fear and intimidation.

"Therefore, it is my hope that this assembly would join with the United States in saying 'no.' No to terror. No to fear. No to intimidation. I ask that all of the member states gathered in this assembly move passage of this resolution, which resolves to sustain the peace of the world and freedom of the people. Thank you. I reserve the remainder of my time for summation."

And with that, Gordon concluded his initial speech. The General Assembly was quiet for a few moments as some of the leaders listened to the translated version of his speech so that they could understand it in their native tongues. After all interpretations were transmitted to the headsets of the members within the delegation, the chairman rose. "Mr. Wade it is your right to reserve for summation. You have one minute and sixteen seconds for your concluding summation. We will now move into technical questions," the chairman announced, as he recognized the delegate from the Republic of China.

The delegate from China arose and asked, "How much will this campaign cost for member states that back your government in its military endeavor?"

Gordon momentarily paused before answering as he always did and said, "The financial aspect of this endeavor is insignificant, as America requests primarily the moral support of member states that move for passage of this resolution."

Moving along in the technical questions, the chairman recognized the delegate from Yugoslavia. The Yugoslavian delegate stood and asked, "In moving for passage of this resolution, will the

United States expect for those member states that voted for passage to add to the military force that will fight terrorist regimes in the Middle East?"

Gordon paused and answered, "No, any military assistance from allied nations will be greatly appreciated; however, we do not expect that any nation support our endeavor with their military."

This time the chairman called upon Russia. The Russian delegate stood and asked, "Is implementing nuclear warheads a possibility in America's war against terrorism?"

The president allowed a very short gap in silence and replied, "Absolutely not. Use of weapons of mass destruction is out of the question entirely." He said this with so much insistence that his claim seemed so honest.

The next nation to pose a technical question was Canada, America's best friend (or rather unofficial flunky). "Does the United States have an exact list of terrorist regimes and locations that will be targeted for this military campaign?"

There was the customary pause, and then the confident response. "Yes."

The chairman called for the last member state of the UN to pose its question. This member state was Pakistan.

"Does the United States intend to infringe upon to the anti-war policy that the United Nations stands upon for the good of maintaining peace amongst nations?"

"No. However, I believe that would be a good topic to be discussed in con-pro debate," answered the president coolly after Pakistan's harsh shot at the US's resolution.

The chairman moved on the procession. "We have reached the end of the technical questions period. We will know move into con-pro debate. I have a con speaker from the Republic of Angola and a pro speaker from the United Kingdom."

The delegate from the Republic of Angola stood and in quite good English began. "May I address the patron of this resolution with a question and reserve my right to address the floor afterward?"

"The patrons do so yield, and that is your right," allowed the chairman as a matter of course.

The delegate from Angola then stated his con argument. "Thank you, Mr. Chairman. Patron, you stated earlier in technical questions that the inquiry concerning the infringement upon the anti-war clause of the United Nations' Charter would better be discussed in con-pro debate. Could you expound on this infringement of the peace clause matter?"

"Of course," answered Gordon politely, although still wearing his frown. He continued, "The anti-war clause of the United Nations is meant as an article of prevention to restrict nations from engaging in war, which has the horrendous effects of unnecessary death. It has been accepted among the member states of the UN that all nations can solve conflicts in a room through communication rather than with guns and bombs on the battlefield. It is to be emphasized that the anti-war clause applies to sovereign nations.

"Let it be noted that the United States does not wish to wage war upon a nation. The United States wishes to apply the use of force upon religious regimes which are no more sovereign nations than they are benign regimes."

After the president's nicely answered response to the question, the delegate moved on with his speech to the delegates of the floor. "Ladies and gentlemen of the Assembly, it is the belief of Angola that a nation's proposal of military force is not to be entertained in the United Nations no matter what the given situation may be. We are to be united in the name of peace and freedom for shared advantage. We believe that this issue between the United

States and the attacking terrorist regimes can be worked out without the sacrifice of lives and needless causalities. The United States has not attempted to seek council on their issue.

"Furthermore, the United States has not tried the regimes in the International Court of Justice. There has not been any type of attempted mediation with the regimes, which America presumes it was attacked by. Thank you. I urge failure of this resolution and yield my time."

"The Republic of Angola has yielded its time. We will now hear from the United Kingdom," the chairman announced. The British delegate stood in proper English fashion and began with an apt British accent.

"May I reserve the right to address the General Assembly and yield my remaining time to France," requested the British delegate.

"Yes, you may, and that is your right," the chairman allowed.

"Members of the Assembly, it is important to realize the weight of the situation at hand. We are not deliberating over measures to avoid terrorist threats. We are not voting on a resolution to liberate a terrorist threatened country. Today, we are voting on a resolution that will help secure the security of all of our nations. The Baricon terrorist regime has taken thousands of American lives, clearly violating many international laws and regulations. The Baricon has committed a crime against humanity.

"However, we cannot hold a trial or attempt to try the leaders of this organization like the twentieth century trials of Nuremberg, because we are fighting an evil that hides behind the fact that it is not a nation but a religious party. It hides behind its masked faces and secret rosters. They hide in caves, bunkers, and other underground places around the globe, primarily in the Middle Eastern region. They have committed a crime, and they must pay the consequence for their wicked actions.

"Wrong is wrong, delegates of the Assembly. What the Baricon has done is simply just that: wrong. As a peace keeping union, we must exterminate that which is not of peace and cannot be made into a peaceful body. They have shown through their actions on November 9th that they do not wish to talk their problems out. Force is a necessity to protect our people from the atrocious effects of terror. If they will do it to one nation, they will do it to others. I warn all of you to keep that in mind: If they will do it to one nation, they will do it to your nation. I yield the remainder of my time to France."

"France, you have thirty seconds," informed the chairman.

"May I reserve my right to address the Assembly?" requested France.

"Yes, that is your right."

"I do not have much time to talk; however, I will say this in the short time I do have. We must look at the deeper issue here. We must not be blinded by petty requests to urge failure and such. It is imperative that we stand with the United States, the victims, and help this nation in its time of great need. I yield the remainder of my time to the chair."

"The delegate from France has no remaining time to yield. Are there any con speakers?"

"Motion!" exclaimed the Canadian delegate.

"The Chair will recognize the delegate from Canada. What is your motion?"

"Canada moves that the Assembly move directly into voting procedure via voice acclamation as the premises of practically all con and pro debate have been heard."

"I will entertain that motion. Is there a second?" Quickly, the delegate from Mexico seconded the motion. The chair continued, "If there are any points, motions, or speeches regarding this motion, please state between the raps of the gavel."

"Motion," stated the Pakistani delegate.

"Delegate from Pakistan, please state your motion."

"Pakistan believes there is much to be discussed concerning the matter at hand. We move that the con-pro debate continues on regular course."

"Is there a second?"

Italy came into the picture with a "second."

"If there are any points, motions, or speeches, please state between the raps of the gravel." Nothing was said; therefore, it was time to move into voting procedure for the Pakistani motion. "We will hold the Pakistani motion voting procedure to voice acclamation. All in favor, state 'Aye.' All opposed state 'Nay.' All in favor?" There was a faint bit of "Aye" heard. Maybe ten or eleven delegates wanted to continue the deliberation. Obviously Pakistan did not have the support of the Assembly on its motion. "All opposed?" inquired the chairman. The crowd went wild on this one. "The ears of the chair have it. Pakistan's motion fails. We will hold Canada's motion as passed to avoid redundancy.

"All in favor of passage of the United States' resolution, please state 'Aye.' All opposed, please state, 'Nay.' All in favor?" The crowd went wild again.

"All opposed?" The same ten or eleven delegates made a little noise with the "Nay's," but all in all those for the resolution won it.

"The ears of the chair have it. The United States' resolution passes." After the chairman announced the United States' resolution victory, Gordon still frowned. It was all part of the act. He walked over to all the nearest delegates who had voted for his resolution and shook their hands. He walked slowly out of the General Assembly shaking many more hands. This victory was certainly good in the aspect of keeping the American public appeased. He went to the United Nations, and now practically had the whole world backing him on his military endeavors to stop terror in the Middle East.

CHAPTER XIV

Just south of Centennial Olympic Park in Atlanta, in the news room of the CNN Center, perhaps the most dramatic news of the century was supposed to break. Given any other circumstance, this particular news break never would have supposed to have broken. This broadcast would be juicy and extremely controversial—the key phrase here being "would be."

The way it all worked was simple. All news stations wanted that sizzling hot story, but all news broadcasters were cautious. Some sizzling hot stories could come with a very high price. One of which was the wrath of the FCC. That independent government agency was the ubiquitous governance of television and radio. Ever since its acceptance as a federal administration in 1934, the US government had somewhat of a domineering grip on all media broadcasts. And by "the US government," the President of the United States is meant. The commissioners of the FCC were handily hand picked by the Big Honcho himself. So, more often than not, news breaks were very censored when it contained, in any way, criticism of the president. (Supposedly, this was a measure of national security.) But not this time; the evil, domineering rule of the FCC would be broken today, Alan Dell, the reportedly dead ambassador, hoped.

The video had been already prepared. Dell along with his special guest Robert Parnell were standing in the central control room of the CNN Center watching as their tape was about to air around the world. It cost Dell about 3.5 million, and the head director (who was about to retire anyway) figured that the deal was packaged with a good enough story and even better money—who cared if it was true. The FCC could flip out about it later. The agreement between Alan Dell and the head director at CNN went like this: The DVD would be popped in inside the news room and paused. At this time, the world would have been watching terrorist specialist and professor from Cambridge University, Steve Conklin, on CNN talking about terrorist organizations this, Baricon leaders that. The CNN screens would go to black for a theatrical couple of seconds—the key word here being "would." It would have been the perfect, abrupt attention grabber. Then, the empty desks of the CNN News Room would be shown just as planned. Then, there would be a voice.

"We interrupt your regularly scheduled program to bring you this special news presentation." The screens again would go to black, as the show would just have been about to commence. The play button would have been pressed in the Central Control Room, and the presentation would have begun. However, the FCC caught wind of the tape, and it was banned from being shown for national security reasons—bummer.

The video quality of the DVD was that of any modern digital camcorder. It was not necessarily taped with national TV, professional-grade standards; therefore, the fact that it was not produced by the good folks at CNN was evident. The scene apparently was shot in a conference room somewhere. There were two men sitting at the end of a long cherry wood table, one of which would have looked amazingly familiar to most people watching.

"Hey, that's the old guy that retired from the White House the other day!" some people would say. "Who are those two guys?" others would ask, as they were not presented with name IDs at the bottom of the screen identifying the two gentlemen on their television sets. The two men were in suits, Dell with a red tie, ex-advisor Parnell with a blue one. The tape would begin with Dell starting, unfolding the appalling truth.

"Hello, I am Alan Dell. My autopsy report stated my occupation was an ambassador, my residency in Iraq, and my cause of death as fatal stroke. According to the report, I died at the age of forty-seven a few days ago. Apparently as I sit here, those details are not precisely accurate. They discovered my dead body near a sewer with a plastic bag over my head; evidently, they believed I was murdered. The federal agency that learned of my supposed death tried to cover it up; they didn't succeed. The truth is, I never died. And, as a result, some people in the White House are probably pissing in their pants right now.

"Secrets are about to be uncovered. Many of your questions about the recent terrorist attacks in New York are about to be answered. Along with me, to assist in explaining what you are bout to hear, is retired Central Intelligence Advisor, Robert Parnell."

"Hello. The day before my retirement from office announcement, I was threatened by President Wade. I am about to disclose horrible secrets about the president as well as myself. Some of these secrets shame me, but they must be told."

Dell picked up where Parnell left off. "Ladies and Gentlemen, the harsh truth of the matter is..." He took a breath partly for effect, partly so that he could gulp air. He resumed. "The President of the United States knew about the terrorist attacks before they occurred, and not only did he do nothing to prevent them, but..." He paused again. Taking another breath, he continued. "Not only did he do nothing to prevent the attacks, but President Wade is responsible for the attacks." Dell looked over at the former Central Intelligence Advisor; they exchanged a brief glance and Parnell picked up where the presumably dead ambassador had stopped at.

"This is one of the sad truths that we will reveal tonight," Parnell said. He pulled up a black, leather briefcase from under the conference table. He quickly put in a combination, and then pulled out several sheets of paper. He held the sheets in both hands and tapped them on the table to evenly straighten them out.

"A few weeks ago, I received a letter from a terrorist member in Iraq requesting a private meeting between me and him. Usually, I would have had to verify this sort of meeting with President Wade and the Security Council; however, this gentlemen stated that no one else was to have knowledge about the meeting before, during, or after it took place. For some reason or another, which I am ashamed of, I agreed to the keep the meeting secret in light of certain offers that were made.

"I met a gentleman named Mr. Sharrod in a coffee shop many miles outside DC the next day. In this private meeting I learned of the terrorist attacks that were being plotted against America. I was asked to betray my country. At first, I declined, disbelieving the audacity of Sharrod's request. Then, he gave me a price to betray the United States. Ultimately, I agreed to sell out this nation for twenty million dollars. I have been highly ashamed of my awful decision up until this very day.

"For the twenty million dollars, the task was very simple. I was to deliver a diversion letter to the president and the National Security Council at the White House detailing a false 'secret operation' in Iraq. I did in fact deliver the false letter to the Council— a horrible act treason on my part. I also divulged several highly classified documents about a top-secret satellite program here in the States."

Dell looked sternly at the camera and said, "I have with me several documents that provide proof of President Wade's knowledge and involvement with the terrorist attacks upon the Statue of Liberty and Times Square which caused approximately 6,700 deaths. I will now read a letter given to me from a contact within the Baricon regime in Iraq.

'The locations have been selected for operation 119. The first location is Liberty Island New York, NY 10004. The second location is 165 Broadway New York, NY 10006. The tentative date at which the operation will be enacted is the morning of 9 November. Verify with initials that the date and these locations are approved.'"

Dell looked back up at the camera. "The letter in which I have just read was initialed and dated "GW" on the day of November 9th. The letter was from an Iraqi contact whose name we cannot disclose for obvious reasons."

After Dell's presentation of the letter, Parnell added to the finger-pointing fest. "The day of my retirement, I received a call from a man I believe to have been dead. Ambassador Dell here was secretly investigating the fake, secret operation in which I had reported to the Council. He knew of the betrayal in which I had agreed to commit. Today, along side him, I am attempting to redeem myself by revealing this scandal, the Wade Scandal. It is imperative that the whistle be blown on this, the greatest act of treachery in American history." Parnell paused and then looked at Dell. The unveiling of facts continued to come out one by one. Keeping the shocking revelations coming, Dell spoke again.

"I knew of Advisor Parnell's sad objectives to betray his country. I also knew of the Baricon terrorist organization's affiliation with President Wade. Like I just mentioned, I can not disclose certain names, as those people who I gained intelligence from would face life threatening consequences. I can disclose the truth, however. It's somewhat plain; and I'll start from the beginning.

"According to my secret sources, President Gordon Wade has been a member of the terrorist organization, the Baricon, since his college years when he attended Columbia University. It has been his plan to betray the United States for over twenty-five years. We also have evidence of a financial transfer of monies linking the president and the Baricon leader Ichtiak Nahas.

"The second piece of evidence that we will reveal concerning President Wade's scandal is a transfer statement which shows a connection between a Mr. Nicholas Stellar and a Harold Finch. The two names, which I have just named, don't exist in their passports' stated country of residency. There are no citizens of Ethiopia with the name Nicholas Worthington Stellar. Furthermore, there are no Harold Douglas Finches that reside in India. When the two accounts were set up, so that this monetary transfer could be made, a random check on their backgrounds revealed that these two names were invalid. The CIA did an investigation on finding out who the two real owners of these accounts were. The CIA pulled video records from Credit Suisse, the bank in which the transfer was made through, and identified the two individuals who went to the bank and made the deposits to become members of Credit Suisse. These individuals were identified as a Sharaq Bandigo and an Arsalin Hussein, members of the notorious terrorist regime the Baricon.

"President Wade was presented with these facts about the transaction at the time of his inauguration and stated that because the transfer did not take place in America that it would be an issue in which other countries would have to sort out. When told that this transfer could possibly be a threat to our national security because of unknown monies moving around through different sects of a terrorist organization, President Wade again stated that it was not a domestic issue. He then cancelled the operation; however, it was forwarded to intelligence organizations in Europe.

"Many European intelligence agencies worked together to sort out the illicit money transfer; however, the bottom of the case was never reached by the European intelligence agencies. So, the question remained a mystery for awhile: Where was the money moving to and why? Well, the case soon reached my desk because one of our Marine covert teams was watching the progress of the European agency developments of the illicit money transfer by Bandigo and Hussein. The president signed a document concerning this matter, which I will now read:

'In light of the numerous terrorist threats that the United States of America has received, we feel it is important to observe the actions of terrorist organizations for our own knowledge and safety. According to the intelligence obtained by the Central Intelligence Agency on March 4, 2005, an illicit transfer of money took place between a 1) Nicholas Stellar and a 2) Harold Finch. These two names were further found to be false, and the true identities of the individuals whom made the transfer were identified as a 1) Sharaq Bandigo and a 2) Arsalin Hussein. Both of these individuals were identified as members of the terrorist organization the Baricon. It has been declined that this matter be investigated by

the CIA in the US because the matter concerns people of other
nations and the action does not directly affect the United States.

'However, the files that were developed during the CIA's
investigation before the President Wade's denouncement of the
project were handed over to several European intelligence agencies
and the Switzerland police. It has been agreed by President Wade,
with the signing of this document, that the European investigations
be observed by the US Marines and reports be made by the US
Marines on the daily status of discoveries made on the case.'

"This letter was signed and dated by the President Wade on
March 5, 2005. It was held as highly classified and confidential.
Only I, the president, and a few members of the Joint Chiefs of Staff
have access to this document.

"It was later found out that the president, in several scattered
offshore accounts, had somehow received an amount of $20.7 billion
dollars. Records of this was made available by the Federal Internal
Affairs Agency. These records were mysteriously missing within
twenty-four hours of their filing."

Dell stopped and looked at Parnell, who was outside the
camera frame rotating his neck in full circles. Truly, Parnell had a
decomposing mind. To cancel out any non-believability from the
American public about what they were saying, Dell went to great
lengths with his special editorial precautions to ensure that Parnell's
slowly disintegration mind was not so apparent on tape.

Dell, after the one second glance over at Parnell, continued
the presentation. "What we have just presented before you is
evidence of the president's link between him and the terrorist
organization, the Baricon. Now, we will look at some of the things
taking place at this very time.

"Omar Madani is an under qualified, non experienced
nomination for the new Central Intelligence Advisor in place of

former Advisor Robert Parnell. On paper, one could take a glance at Madani's resume and see that he served in the military for numerous years, has a good educational background, and has held increasingly high positions in the Federal Investigation Bureau. But, all in all, the man is completely and utterly under qualified because he had no political experience or even a professional relationship with President Wade.

"When I was working as an ambassador in Iraq, one of my jobs was to obtain intelligence about inner workings of the government and the political parties that influenced the Iraqi government. The most highly watched political party during my term was—none other than—the Baricon. After interviewing and, to be completely candid, bribing several members of the Baricon about records of secret members and such, I obtained lists of many undercover members of the Baricon to get other coinciding terrorist organizations. After learning of Madani's nomination, I learned that he was on one of my lists as a member of Al Shidad. Al Shidad is a brotherhood organization that practically works under the Baricon. Instead of a brotherhood organization, as they call it, it is rather a father-son relationship between the two organizations, similar to the federal government and the state government here in the US.

"It is unknown as to whether Mr. Madani is privy to the fact that President Wade knew that Mr. Madani is a member of the terrorist regime Al Shidad, but somehow I get the notion they are very good friends via their relationship through their terrorist networks.

"Now, moving on. It is up to the government officials around the country and delegates and leaders around the world to weigh the truth of what we have just presented. We solemnly promise by our names that all of what we have claimed is true. I presented these facts to many federal intelligence bureaus such as the CIA and the

DIA weeks prior to this announcement. The CIA rep the president, and my report was blown off. Als briefed on these shocking facts. They started a secret inves weeks ago, which was brought to a halt after the DIA shooting in Washington and President Wade's obtainment of knowledge about the investigation. It is imperative that there be action taken to stop future plans of terror. Presently, the president is getting ready to depart to the annual World Dinner. It is frightening to think of what his possible plans could be during this time, considering his affiliation with terrorist organizations and so forth. Please take heed to the facts divulged. The future lies with all those who are listening."

And that was going to be the perfect plan. Dell had coughed up the $3.5 million and everything. Agreements were made, unofficial of course (being that this was a money-under-the-table type thing). However, there was just one major problem. As the tape was about to air, the FCC called in talking very aggressively and making some pretty hefty threats.

Someone in the newsroom at CNN had leaked the information about the tape after watching it, and the FCC threatened to press charges on the grounds of slander and this, that, and the other (and, of course, they threw in the fact about the "threat to national security" bit). The head director at CNN backed out at the last moment before the tape was supposed to be aired. Was he even thinking about giving the money back to Dell? Not really. Did he eventually give it up after Dell threatened to release his secretly recorded footage of their under-the-table meeting and accepted bribe? The director agreed saying that Dell's deal was "fair enough."

Dell and Parnell's tape was also beckoned forth by the FCC. They demanded all copies of the DVD including the original. Would the FCC get them? Of course not. Did the FCC make more threats?

Of course they did. Government agencies were all the same. The 'CC took many things very seriously, and this just so happened to be one of those things. They were there to ensure they did what any president-controlled government agency would do—destroy evidence so accounts of history would not be able to mention them, and also so they could keep their jobs and all.

* * *

Parnell and Dell were in the rental Chrysler 300 on the way to Savannah, GA, where they would abandon the car, rent another, drive to Alabama and take a connecting flight somewhere to somewhere to a place in which they would disappear: all measures to get lost, just in case.

"Do you think they are following us?" asked Parnell.

"Could be," answered Dell.

"Where to now?" Parnell asked, not recalling that Dell had just told him.

"Savannah."

"What is there?"

"Another rental."

"Where do we go then?"

"Huntsville."

"I went there once to visit the military base. Lovely place, it is."

"Sure."

"What's in Huntsville?"

"Naked women."

"Considering how much I love naked women, I'd like to return home to be with my wife—for reasons that I can't even explain to myself."

"We'll split up after Huntsville."

"Going where?"

"Wherever you want to go."

"Well, do we send this tape to any other channels?" Parnell asked, not recalling that Dell told him already.

"MSNBC is probably already catching heat from the FCC, so if they don't air it, I'll have to stream it over the Internet. The message won't reach as many people in as short a period of time as it would on TV, but it will certainly spread over time. Time that we don't have."

CHAPTER XV

"Mr. President?"

"Speaking."

"This is Secretary Santiago. We have a bit of a situation."

"Regarding?"

"A tape."

"All right. What tape are we referring to?"

"A tape that was prevented from being aired on the CNN network almost an hour ago."

"Brief me."

"Yes, sir. Former Intelligence Advisor Robert Parnell and a man claiming to be the dead Iraqi ambassador, Alan Dell, tried to leak a tape on the CNN news station. The director in the control room claimed the man who identified himself as Alan Dell attempted to bribe him to put their tape on the air."

"Really? How much did he offer?"

"I hear the amount was in the seven figures."

"Wow. Cash?"

"He did not provide the method of payment in the FCC report."

"The FCC blew the whistle on it?"

"The FBI, also."

"What was on the tape?"

"It's appalling, Mr. President. From what I hear, the so-called resurrected Ambassador Dell and ex-advisor Parnell alleged on the tape that you were secretly involved with terrorist organizations. I've been informed that they not only stated that you knew about the terrorist attacks in New York City but that you practically ordered them. The claims are really outrageous. According to the FCC, there were claims by Mr. Parnell that you forced him to retire. They say in the tape that he admitted to bribes from terrorist organizations but ultimately decided not to be a part of it or something to that effect. The FCC told us that this guy who claims to be Alan Dell looks similar to the one that died, but are not completely certain if it is him. They said that Mr. Dell accused you of involvement in a twenty billion dollar transaction with members of a terrorist regime."

"I didn't know I obtained billions from terrorists. No one tells me anything anymore." Gordon laughed. This news of the tape was almost making him nervous.

"Yes, but the FCC and FBI are jointly investigating the tape to gain more information regarding the allegations and legitimacy of the claims."

"Legitimacy of the claims?! Parnell isn't all there in the head as we all know. He's a fruit cake. 'Forced to retire'? Is that what he said? He retired because his doctor advised him to do so. There doesn't need to be an investigation. Can you believe this malarkey these guys are pulling?"

"I'm as shocked as you, Mr. President."

"I want you to make sure the entire departments of the FCC and FBI which are handling this case are put under a gag order. I want everyone evolved signed to binding contracts to keep this matter suppressed. This is the last thing we need during these chaotic times with the terrorist attacks in New York. People are always trying to stir up confusion and spread mass disarray. This is one of the worst press stunts I have ever heard of in my career. It is almost unbelievable what people will do."

"Like I said, it's really appalling."

"All right, here's what I want you to do, also. I want you to get me all the specifics on that tape. My flight to Zurich is supposed to leave in about thirty minutes. I want a full fledged report from you within the next ten minutes. And one more thing. How many copies of the tape are there, and who has them?"

"I'm not sure, sir."

"Call me back with that information."

"Yes, sir."

"All right. Goodbye." Gordon hung up the phone. He sat in the Oval office stock-still. Waiting.

His phone rang ten minutes later. Expectedly, it was State Secretary Santiago again. "Hello, Mr. President, I have some new facts regarding the Parnell and Dell video."

"First, don't regard to it as that anymore, and tell everyone down at the FCC and the Bureau, as well. Calling it 'the tape' will be just fine. I'm sure I'll know what you're talking about."

"Yes, sir."

"So, how much was the bribe for?"

"Which one, sir?"

"What do you mean which one?"

"Well, there was the bribe that former advisor Parnell claimed that he had received from a terrorist regime; the other was a bribe which the CNN director was offered."

"Give me both."

"Well, the former advisor claimed that he had received twenty million dollars from the Baricon regime to deliver that letter he read in our Security Council meeting a few days ago. He claimed he was bribed by a member of the Baricon and received a money wire. He claimed that he knew the Baghdad Project never existed in the first place."

"Well, we know that."

"He also admitted to his under-the-table divulging of blueprints that detailed our X-900 satellite project to a member of the Baricon. The other bribe was the bribe offered to the CNN control room director which was for over three million dollars from Alan Dell."

"You don't have a precise dollar amount from this Dell poser?"

"In the report that the FBI gave him to fill out, he simply stated that he was offered a few million. I made a call a few minutes ago and learned that the bribe was over three million."

"Some of this doesn't add up."

"Not much of it does."

"Did you get those gag orders sent out? And does everyone understand the high level of confidentiality in this matter?"

"Yes, everyone who knows about the tape has been advised on the level of confidentially in which they are now under. Written confidentiality agreements are being sent via e-mail as we speak from the Department of Justice."

"Does the Department of Justice know about the tape?"

"No, sir. They have simply been asked to form a contract that binds everyone in the FCC and FBI whom is working the tape investigation to secrecy over every matter they have worked during the course of the last and next twenty-four hour periods."

"All right. I'm about to leave for Zurich. Send me more up-to-the-minute reports via e-mail. Make sure CNN is being properly pressed. I don't even want to hear a hint about the tape."

"It will be done, sir."

"And keep other news networks like MSNBC on watch. I want all their news bulletin considerations monitored. If anything is heard about any media attempting to put this news out there, put a lid on them.

"Yes, sir."

"Goodbye."

Gordon rose from his chair and stretched out a bit. It would be a long day, surely. He had to go to the World Dinner, kidnap all the world leader's wives, and get the world leaders to surrender all of their nuclear arms—a day in the life of the president. He called Effie, his favorite assistant, to get an update on the attendance list. As he stood, he buzzed for her from his desk phone. She quickly answered before the second ring.

"Good afternoon, Mr. President, how may I help you?"

"How many times do I have to tell you Effie? You don't have to call me Mr. President. Master Wade is just fine."

"Yes, sir, Mr. Master Wade, sir," said Effie, slightly giggling more out of politeness rather than perceived humor.

"You need to say it with a little more enthusiasm than that, Ef. Come on. I don't know why I deal with this. You're fired."

"Oh no, what do I do now?"

"Clear your desk, immediately. That's precisely what. On the contrary, in all actuality, I cannot get rid of you, though. I need you to keep all the nagging Senators and Representatives out of my office. They actually believe you when you say I'm sick."

"Okay. I'm grateful I serve such purpose around here. You're quite the convincer."

"So, Effie, how's the attendance role looking for the World Dinner tomorrow?"

"As of now, I have not received any memos or letters indicating cancellation for tomorrow's World Dinner."

"Well, that's good, I suppose. Can you tell them I'm sick, so I unfortunately won't be able to make it?"

"Would you like me to prepare a doctor's note, also?"

Gordon laughed. "That's why I keep you around, Ef. No, I think I'll go."

"All right, 'Mr. Master Wade,' sir. Did I have enough enthusiasm that time around?"

"Yes, that was sufficient. Well, Ef, I got to go but I want you to keep me posted on the attendance via my text messages. Let me know if anyone cancels for tomorrow.

"Alright."

"Thanks, Ef," Gordon said as he pressed his finger on the "Line 1" button on the phone and disconnected. He grabbed his personal undisclosed, unnumbered cell phone from the bottom drawer of his oak wood desk. He pressed "Direct Connect" and made the call. The phone rang twice before there was an answer.

"*Halaw*," Nahas answered.

"*Marhabtayn*. Are we sparing the formalities, today?"

"No need for formalities. We are brothers, and it is a beautiful day."

"Everything is going as planned, but there is one problem. Are you sure we finished the job on Ambassador Dell there in Iraq?" Gordon inquired.

"Yes, he is gone."

"What did the boys down there do with the body?"

"They disposed of it."

"Via..."

"He was incinerated like the rest."

"So, you did not actually see the body?"

"Well, we do not set aflame bodies in my palace. What has occurred?"

"I have reason to believe that Alan Dell may still be alive."

"Impossible. He has been gone for days."

"Did you witness his death?"

"Mr. Wade, you have nothing to worry about. Alan Dell is not alive. I assure you that he has been taken care of."

"I have just received a brief that a tape has been made with our friend Mr. Dell talking."

"I assure you that there is no such matter to worry about. In America, they make counterfeit tapes and images all of the time. This Dell imposter, what was he talking about?"

"I have not yet seen the tape. I may not be able to view it for a few hours. I have to attend our little engagement for tonight."

"May Allah watch over you. You will receive much blessing. I feel it in my spirit."

"Thank you, brother. I feel it in my spirit, as well. In the brief in which I just received regarding the tape, one of my contacts informed me that the Mr. Dell poser claimed that he did not in deed die, and furthermore declares that I am associated with the Baricon regime."

Nahas was silent for a moment. "Do not worry. I see great fortune for you," he said as the conversation was thus concluded.

Gordon disconnected and sat back down at his desk. He stared at the door in front of him as he meditated, or rather, daydreamed on the upcoming deeds of the night. He folded his arms behind his head and meditated deeper.

Then, there was a knock at the door. He walked over to the door to open it, not really expecting but wondering if it was his own CIA agents standing at the door ready to put him in cuffs for high treason and breach of presidential oath. He sighed, "*Alia iact est,*" as he reached for the door knob. Fortunately, it was not the CIA, the DIA, the FBI, or Internal Affairs. It was his wife. She had a mountain of luggage accompanying her. She had her mandatory Dooney & Bourke carrying bag and a couple of Louis Vuitton suitcases.

"Ready for the trip?" she asked, giving off her trademark beam that Gordon had missed for the past couple of days.

"Ah, there's that smile!" They kissed passionately for a moment. Partially, this kiss of passion was based on Gordon's realization that this may be one of the last kisses he would be able to give her. "You look beautiful," he noted, his breath taken.

She was dressed in one of her many incredibly stylish outfits. She was wearing a black shawl over a white blouse with khaki slacks for the trip. Today was Burberry and the ensemble looked marvelous on her, all of it especially made for the First Lady. Her hair was down and flowing stunningly. Stunning, she absolutely was.

He had the impulse, which he had so often felt, to just break down and confess to her everything, all of it. *Dear, I'm going to kidnap all the world leaders' wives tomorrow and hold the leaders hostage until they reach each and any one of my demands,* he wanted to tell her. It would break her heart. *Dammit!* He had waited too long. He always had a plan; however, for this particular situation, he was drawing continuous blanks in the plan department.

"You look gorgeous. I am... speechless."

"Thanks, Mr. President. And you, too."

He jokingly emulated a mute man who could not speak, making mouth movements with no words actually coming out."

"You're so silly."

He was continuing to lip-sync, maintaining his emulation of a voiceless man. She was laughing; he was smiling.

"Well, say something."

He was still moving his soundless lips and then said, "I can't. Can't you see I'm speechless?"

"I see. Well, speechless husband, are you ready for our rendezvous. Our Secret Service friends are waiting for us to go."

"Okay. Hey, are you sure you want to go. You know you don't have to. I'll understand."

"I know, and thanks for being so understanding. I'm coping. I think I'm pulling back into the loop. Now isn't a time to be timid, but to be courageous. Kinda like you, chief."

"Aw shucks. Thanks."

"Really, I mean it. I married a good one. You are the definition of a great man, dear. And you should note that I do in fact love you more."

"Sorry, dear. I am unable to concur with you in that regard."

"I do. You just don't know."

"No, you just don't know." With that statement made by Gordon, he knew he was speaking volumes. *She really didn't know.* She had no idea. Why hadn't he just told her sooner. Oh, yeah, it was the whole killing him in cold blood thing, he remembered.

"Yes, I do," she said practically singing the "do." "I'll show you how much more throughout the duration of our Zurich trip." *Dammit*, Gordon thought again. Sadly, it was highly probable, or more so inevitable, that he would not have the opportunity to reap the benefits of her offer regarding her demonstration of how much more she loved him throughout the duration of the trip.

"I certainly am looking forward to that."

"And I, also."

"Shall we?" he offered as he stuck out his elbow and hooked his arm forming a gap for her to stick her arm through. Arm in arm, he escorted her to Air Force One.

PART IV

THE CONCLUSION

CHAPTER XVI

Patrick's room in the Hotel Adler came equipped with the standard Swiss hotel package of a telephone, television set, safe, radio, mini bar, hairdryer, ventilation system, shower and bath, modem connections, and soundproof windows. His temporary living quarters in Zurich wasn't too shabby. It was not the Hotel Baur Au Lac like the president would be staying in; however, that was okay, because Patrick, like most assassins, was not too picky about hotel accommodations.

The Hotel Adler was located in the heart of the Niederdorf area of Zurich. It was a three star hotel with five stories, fifty-two rooms, and a nice restaurant down by the lobby. Patrick was staying on the third floor of the hotel with a window view overlooking a little street called Rosengasse. Although, he knew every surrounding street, all of the key tourist locations, the population, and pretty much everything else about the new city he found himself in, he was not minding any of that at the time. He was cleaning his gun—or some would call it a cell phone.

It was the newest advancement in covert firearms on the black market. It was called the NEXKIA 22. It was originally manufactured by the Japanese underground about a month ago and on the global black market for about eight thousand dollars. The United States Secret Service and the FBI didn't even know about this firearms advancement yet.

The cell phone gun, as it was popularly called, could discharge five small bullets in rapid succession before reloading—and before a security guard could react to the discovery that what he thought was a normal cell phone was actually a pistol. Concealed inside the phone were a revolving cylinder, a firing mechanism, and a 1.75-inch gun barrel. The muzzle was positioned near the cell phone's battery pack. With a press of the button 4, 5, or 6 the cell phone gun could be cocked. With a press of the button 1 or 3, it could be fired.

The NEXKIA 22 had an outer cover made of plastic and a lethal firing interior, which was also made of plastic. It was practically undetectable by most metal detectors.

"Clean," he said as he closed the back of his once used NEXKIA 22. He walked over to the wooden desk in the corner of the room where he had laid out a map of the city of Zurich earlier. He picked up his pen and dabbled a bit on the map, plotting the entrance and getaway. This assassination, accounts of history would most certainly mention in bold print and highlights in textbooks and reference materials. His name as the assassin, history would not mention. Patrick was still THE best.

His gun phone rang on the bed. He walked over to his white, cotton-sheeted bed, picked up the phone, and answered in passable German, *"Guten Tag."*

It was Alan Dell. *"Guten Morgen. Wie geht es Ihnen?"* (English: Good morning. How are you?).

"Es geht. Was möchten Sie?" (I'm okay. What do you want?)

"Folgen Sie unseren Plänen?" (Is everything going according to our plans?)

"Ja." (Yes.)

There was a small gap of silence. *"Sind Sie nervös um heute Abend?"* (Are you nervous about tonight?)

"Nein. Meine einzige Angst ist Angst." (No. My only fear is fear).

"Gut. Bis spatter." (Good. Talk to you later.)

"Auf Wiedersehen," Patrick said, hanging up.

* * *

Back in America, it was 1 a.m. on a moonlit night. A driving Alan Dell and a sleeping Robert Parnell had just got off of Highway 75 and merged onto Highway 16 South coming from Atlanta to Savannah when Dell had hung up with Patrick. Illuminated by their Chrysler's headlights, the Georgian landscape made for a picturesque ride through the rural areas of the state. They were now about three and a half hours from their next destination. *I wonder how much it will cost me for calling Zurich,* Dell wondered. He maintained focus on the road and hit a few bumps on purpose in an attempt to awaken Parnell who was snoring extremely loud.

Dell drove, saw a bump, hit it—no success. Parnell could probably sleep off the entire trip. The sleeping old man was virtually of no use now that the tape had been made. He contemplated stopping, kicking Parnell out of the car, and leaving the old Sleeping Beauty out on the side of the road. Think anyone would notice the ex-Central Intelligence Advisor to the President if he was slung out on the shoulder of the Georgian highway? *Probably not,* Dell thought.

Shifting mental attention from Parnell's loud snoring, Dell thought about the tape. He was almost certain that the tape would go on the air. On no other channel would their claims have been perceived as legitimate by TV watchers. There was always MSNBC, but if they couldn't get it on CNN, getting it on the other channel was almost as highly likely to be highly unlikely. The FCC had screwed them over big time. In America, where expression was supposed to be permitted and speech supposed to be allowed, the government outfit that called itself the "FCC" stood to block freedom of expression and speech just in case the government did not like what was being said. The government was really liking President Wade, more so perhaps than any other president in history, so whatever President Wade liked, the government liked. That guy could get away with murder—oh, yeah, that was his plan, Dell recalled. But, it was true. Sadly enough, President Wade was getting away with the murder of thousands of Americans, treason, and numerous other criminal counts which included conspiracy and things of that sort. *He could not possibly get away with it, could he?*

Yellow lines passed and came, passed and came. Dell drove and thoughts concurrently passed and came. He would have to leak it on the Internet. How else would he leak it? Internal Affairs? They would think it was joke; then, they would show it to President Wade and see what he thought about it. Internal Affairs, of course, was supposed to monitor the activities of the president, ideologically. Was that the case? Far from it. The president set himself up through the past months of being in office, ensuring that all aspects of the White House, government, and, in a way, the world were under his reign. He even had his fingers in the Food and Drug Administration. For what? It did not have necessarily anything to do with helping to ensure that the food and drugs in the country were healthy, it was to simply have power; Dell huffed at this notion. How did he get to

such a position of power? *How had he deceived a whole nation,*
Dell pondered infuriately as he watched the lines on the Highway 16
pass and come, pass and come.

Parnell, still sleep, turned his head away from the window
side of the passenger seat making it so that his sleeping head was
facing Dell. He ceased snoring. Dell rejoiced, for the old man had
stopped snoring and carrying on bronchial tube ruckus. Dell had to
bring an end to his internal, joyous celebration when Parnell made
one of the loudest snoring noises ever produced in the history of
mankind. Dell slammed on the brake; this would surely wake up old
Sleepy from his slumber. As the car yanked to a halt, Parnell's eyes
opened widely like a deer under headlights.

"Wh-what's going on?"

"Nothing. A car just pulled out in front of me, that's all."

"Oh, I thought we hit something," Parnell said as he closed
his eyes, continuing in his dormant undertakings of dreams and
more snoring. What had this old guy been through that would drive
him to be this heavy-eyed? Old age, Dell thought in response to his
question. Then, he noticed something—the bright lights from the
vehicle behind him.

The white pickup truck behind him had been trailing them
for quite some time. It seemed odd to Dell, because usually if
someone slammed on their brake as hard as he did, a person would
honk and/or switch lanes. He glanced at his rearview for a few
moments. He would have asked Parnell if he had noticed the vehicle,
but of course, the tired, old man had been catching up on a lifetime of
snooze in the Chrysler rental.

Dell turned his right blinker on and merged over to the left
lane, looking in his rearview checking out the white pickup truck.
Was he being overly suspicious? His line of work and the situation
that he found himself in certainly warranted his (perhaps extreme)

precautions. The white pickup stayed in the far left lane at a continuous speed, diagonally pursuing Dell and Parnell. Dell watched, and after about a minute of watching, his suspicious thoughts were intensified as the pickup truck slid over a lane, again finding itself behind Dell and Parnell.

Do I speed up? Do I keep going at this same speed and direction, he questioned. He looked over at Parnell—still sleep. He looked in his rearview at the white pickup—still following. He looked at the lines on the road—still passing and coming, passing and coming. The idea of stopping popped in his head but quickly popped out. The question of *who?* entered his head quite late, but it made itself a pretty big nest in the inquiry sector of his brain as he contemplated speeding, getting off at the exit, or both. He looked at Parnell again, thinking that the old man should not get the pleasure of being able to sleep through this whole scenario.

"Parnell," he said, but got absolutely, positively, completely no response or a winch of an eyebrow. There was no facial or bodily movement. He called his name again louder. "Parnell!" He tapped him on the shoulder, and if the old man was not snoring, Dell would not have known that he was still alive. He tapped him again a little more aggressively, almost punching his shoulder. Nothing. He shook him a bit and finally seemed to have gained some kind of reaction from old Sleeping Beauty. "Rise and shine, buddy," Dell said.

"Are we there yet?" Parnell asked. Of course, he sounded dazed and confused, as was not usual.

"No, but it seems as though we have some friends who want to follow us tonight."

"Where?" Parnell inquisitively asked, moving his head as though he was about to turn to look behind him.

"Keep facing ahead. I don't want them to know we know they're following us."

"And how did you arrive to the conclusion that someone was following us?"

"Don't worry about it. Just keep your eyes looking forward."

"Just be reasonable, Alan. I've worked thirty years in national security and twenty years in the Army; you don't think I know a little something about detection? Pull over. It's interesting watching you act like some sort of spy. You're a politician, or rather an openly decisive idiot."

Dell ignored Parnell and kept driving, still glancing up at the rearview mirror. Dell had saved Parnell's life, and in return for his gratitude, the old man was calling him an openly decisive idiot.

Now, was not the time for insults or needless bickering with the old fool, Dell decided, continuing to look at the rearview. The white pickup seemed to stick pretty close to their Chrysler as the two vehicles were drifting at about sixty-five mph down the highway.

"You ever go to school?" Parnell inquired again.

Dell looked at Parnell, back at the road, then back at the rearview—white truck still there. He switched lanes again.

"You receive secondary education?" Parnell asked.

"Yes."

"An American school?"

"Yes."

"Figures. What was your IQ? Was it a negative number?" Dell didn't even look over at the old man this time and just kept driving. The white pickup switched over behind them into their same lane again. They certainly were not trying to be secretive about following.

"It doesn't appear as though they're trying to be stealth," commented Dell, almost to himself.

"Pull over. Just trust me."

Suddenly, they felt a big jolt. The pickup had bumped them from behind. Dell sped up. "Our worst fear has just been confirmed." The white pickup was not far behind, picking up speed as well. Both the vehicles were moving at about ninety mph fifteen seconds after the bump.

"Our day just seems to get progressively better as it goes on," Parnell threw in to break the dramatic, theatrical, high-speed-car-chase silence.

"Doesn't it seem like."

"Who do you think it is?"

"I'm willing to bet it's your friends from the Baricon. I doubt federal agents would go to these measures. They would have just pulled us over."

"It's DIA," Parnell said.

"And what makes you assume that?"

"Instinct, I presume."

"Instinct?" Dell said as though expecting more to follow. Why he expected more to follow in a statement made by the man with the disintegrating mind, he did not know.

The white pickup behind them sped up and pulled up beside them. The tinted windows prevented both Dell and Parnell from seeing inside the truck. "That's a dark tent. Limo windows don't even come that opaque," Dell observed, speeding up. The pickup sped to a faster speed. Dell wished he would have picked the Porsche at the Hertz Rental. Why had he gone with the cheaper buy?

The pickup forced itself over into the lane that Dell and Parnell were in, causing them to slide over onto the shoulder of the highway. "Bloody Mary, these blokes are serious, aren't they," Parnell said in a matter-of-fact tone.

"Looks like it. Hold on."

"I must ask the inevitable question at this juncture. What do you suggest I hold on to? My old, bloody family jewels?" The white truck crashed itself into the Chrysler again, causing Dell to lose control of the vehicle. The Chrysler rental sped into the four-foot concrete median on the side of the highway. It almost went through the concrete. The crashing Chrysler halted after moving a substantial amount of the concrete out of place as a result of the pickup truck's assailment. What a debacle Dell and Parnell found themselves in as they rolled along with the car.

A horrible "accident" had occurred. The pickup truck stopped and pulled over in front of the crashed Chrysler and called the ambulance. "There has just been a horrible accident," one of the three Middle Eastern men said as he got out of the pickup and walked towards the wrecked Chrysler.

After the Baricon operative on the cell phone hung up with the dispatcher, he walked over to where the scene of the vehicular "accident" had taken place. Dell and Parnell were not moving in their seats. A lot of blood was streaming from the faces of the two individuals who were so terribly affected by the accident. Seeing how sadly terrible and painfully effected the two were as they lay there, the driver of the pickup accompanied the other two operatives in sliding the two out of the car and kicking the living mess out of them behind the sideways turned car so that passing cars could not witness the merciless beating they were bestowing. The principle of never kick a man while he's down was not applied as they continued to kick the bodies pitilessly.

After they finished kicking and stomping any bit of life left in the two crash-contorted human beings, a red van slowed up on the side of the road near the "accident." There was a middle-aged brunette lady in the van who asked what happened.

"It was a horrible accident," one of the Baricon operatives responded as if shocked by the scene he had caused.

"Do you need to call the police?"

"No, we already called them. Thanks anyway, though."

"All right. Have a good night," the lady in the van said, pulling off. More cars came and stopped by to offer help, and all were declined their offer to volunteer help. About five minutes later, an ambulance came storming down Highway 16 going the opposite direction that the crash had taken place. Passing the vehicular crash, the ambulance turned the vehicle around going through a gap in the concrete median that divided the two directions of the highway about a quarter of a mile up from the accident. When the ambulance arrived to the scene, the self-proclaimed "victims" told the meds that the Chrysler had swerved into their lane, hit their car, and drove crazily of the highway into the concrete wall.

"These two are dead," one of the EMTs reported to the Baricon tri-team. Mission accomplished, they thought.

"What?! Oh, no!" was the gathered shocked response given off by the group as they rejoiced in their heads as they had certainly finished the job.

"Since deaths have occurred, police are on the way. When they get here, you will have to go down to the police station and give a statement. It's just procedure. I'm sorry this had to happen."

The three went down to the Greene County Sheriff's Department to give their statements. After giving their innocent testimonies of how they were the "victims" of the fatal accident, they were released. They were free men, and they would get a bonus for this one. They had recovered the only remaining copy of the tape, as well.

CHAPTER XVII

Throughout the course of history, it has been amazing how nature could be completely impartial to human activities and events. In the midst of the tragedy and mourning in America, the world somehow found a way to continue. Earth, in some mysterious way, kept its course and still rotated around the sun. It was a sheer miracle.

* * *

This was particularly evident in the sunny and blisteringly cold country of Switzerland. A wide array of people of diverse nationalities rejoiced at the World Dinner Banquet. It was the annual event in which all the leaders of the world gathered in one place for a celebration of world peace. Iraq was a no show: big surprise, surprise, seeing as all of their political leaders were rapidly fleeing around the world as they were catching blame for the attacks in New York. The USA was in attendance and full manifestation represented by Mr. and Mrs. President Wade along with the entourage of Secret Service agents. Also present were Mr. and Mrs. Prime Minister from Great Britain, Mr. and Mrs. Chief of State from China, Mr. and Mrs. Premier from Russia, and all the rest of the Big Dogs and their spouses from around the world.

It was a slightly overcast, chilly autumn night. The wind provided a slight breeze that steadily moved through the Swiss hills. The scene at the World Dinner was utterly picturesque. Gordon appeared before the cameras with his wife. He was blending with the rest of the gentlemen, wearing a black tuxedo. Mrs. Wade was fashionably dressed wearing an elegant, black dress and a white mink coat. She had a pink flower pinned in her hair, which was the finishing touch to her four hour hairstyle preparation. She wore her clothes and hairstyle well but herself even better. When she stepped out of the Cruiser with her husband, all the leaders and even their wives stopped and practically gawked at her. How beautiful, everyone thought. She gracefully made her may through the lights, the cameras, and the noise which seemed to slightly subside when she stepped on the scene outside the entrance of the World Dinner. She flashed that glowing smile like she always did. How revered she was for both her beauty and her grace.

Gordon was even slightly thrown off when they met minutes before their catwalk after she finished her Swiss hair solon appointment. She looked so amazing, he thought as his thoughts of kidnapping all the world leaders and their wives were temporarily put on hold. Yes, it would soon turn into a really, really ugly night, he realized; however, for now, it was simply splendid.

Mr. Madani appeared out of the woodworks when the president exited the Cruiser and gave Gordon a nod to let him know everything was going as planned. Gordon almost didn't notice Madani's nod, which was minuscule in his mind, as he was overpowered by the thought of her. *Damn, my wife looks good.* He thought of her beauty, and then he cursed himself. He had procrastinated and he had never gotten around to telling her. Procrastination was a lame excuse that he kept repeating in his mind in an attempt to justify not telling her the truth. Well, she would find out tonight. He cursed himself in his head more. Stopped. Then, he cursed the fact in his mind over again. As he was doing all of this cursing in his mind, he was escorting Mrs. Wade across the red carpet. He was smiling and waving at the crowd. Smiling and waving, then smiling and waving more. He had his hand partially cupped as he moved it from side to side, as that was the official American president wave.

* * *

Coming in from another entrance with His NEXKIA 22 in pocket, Patrick walked into the Zurich Commons Center with his cell phone fully loaded. Once through the glass revolving entrance doors, he approached the security checkpoint in front of the escalators which led to the World Dinner Banquet. He didn't flinch at the sight of the surveillance cameras which practically covered the ceiling, surveying every angle and viewpoint of the Commons Center.

He was dressed in a cheap, black suit with a cheap, blue tie and fake alligator boots which screamed "Hello, I am a member of the press." Of course like any member of the press, he had a camera strapped around his neck, basically the only thing not cheap—because the media company he worked for supplied it, of course. Dressed the part (very convincingly), he approached the security checkpoint.

Security was tight (and fittingly so). It was the World Dinner where the most powerful individuals in the world came to stuff their faces and take pictures with their wives at a benefit that helped support world peace. Peace, benevolence, and good morality, what all world leaders were about, supposedly.

Patrick was standing in line in front of a metal detector, sixteenth person away from the checkpoint. *Many cameras*, he thought, not flinching at the surveillance display of the seemingly hundreds of cameras. *An immense amount of security, minuscule amount of exit doors*, he thought taking in the environment. Now, fifteenth in line, he toyed around with the camera as if he was really doing something a professional photographer would do to a camera. At random, he toyed around with the flash settings on it. Dropping his camera back down to a hanging position on his chest, having shuffled around with it for about four or five minutes, he was seventh away from passing through security checkpoint in line. When he looked up from his camera, it opened him up to a very social reporter standing behind him.

"William Law, London Press Report," the man said, holding his hand out with a smile. He had beady eyes, a wrinkled forehead, and a skinny face. He was also wearing a cheap suit.

"Larry McAllen, Inside Out Canada Online," Patrick said as he reluctantly shook the reporter's hand. Then, he turned back around facing forward again.

"Canada, huh?"

"Yes. Canada," Patrick said, still looking forward.

"Good hockey there. It can get a bit cold here in Switzerland. Tell me, which would you say was colder during this time of year?"

Patrick had a slight disgusted look on his face as he was facing forward away from this very sociable gentleman. "This is my first time in Switzerland. I wouldn't know."

"Really? It's a beautiful country isn't it?"

"Yes, it's alright," Patrick said maintaining his forward stance, attempting to acknowledge the Englishmen behind him as little as possible. He now had only one person in front of him in the metal detector security line.

"Finally! They act as if the Prime Minister was in there or something," William law said sarcastically.

"As if," Patrick said moving right along. It was his turn to go through the machine. The security guard summoned him, holding out a basket for Patrick to place all the metal objects he had his cheap reporter's suit.

Patrick pulled off his camera and put it in the basket. His fake passport, change, rental car keys, self-made press pass, pen, and his NEXTEL 22 all went into the basket. The guard examined the contents in the basket, as Patrick walked through the detector. He went through and the alarm went off. The guard spoke some German words Patrick could not entirely make out. He could make out the words "legs" and "here." The guard pointed to the place where he wanted Patrick to stand. Patrick presumed that the guard was trying to get him to spread his arms and legs so he could be manually checked by the guard. He spread his legs and held his arms out as the guard waved the hand detector up and down his body. The detector went off near the front of his face, and Patrick quickly opened his mouth to display his silver crown on one of his right molars so the guard could note that it was just his tooth crown making the alarm go off. What sensitive detectors.

Patrick was cleared and walked toward the escalator toward the pressroom with the demeanor *I'm with press, supposed to be here, been to a million of these.* He certainly had been to many of these—assassinations, that was. This would be his last—he hoped by choice rather than by the confines of a prison. And this time, the Baricon would not come to him for another assassination; he was betraying them, and he would completely disappear after he had done his little deed here at the World Dinner.

He rode the escalator with the, at least, fifty other people on it. He blended in nicely with his camera hanging from his neck, pen behind his ear, cheap suit on. Once he made it up the escalator, he walked over to the hostess standing in the middle of the crowded lobby. "Do you speak any English?" he asked.

"Yes, sir. How may I help you?" she chimed with a Swiss accent, giving off a mechanical smile which she was required to give to everyone through the duration of the night.

"Where is the press area?" he asked. All of a sudden someone slammed a hand on his shoulder. His instinct was to immediately grab the hand, flip the assailant, and slam his foot into the assailant's chest, pinning the attacker down. He hesitated before reacting.

"Hey, mate, you going to the press area? It's right over here," announced the voice of the assailant, who turned out to be the annoyingly friendly English reporter, Mr. William Law.

"Mr. Law," Patrick said as he turned around to face him. "After you."

"It's right this way. I remember you saying this was your first time in Switzerland, so I figured you might not know where to go. They put us in the same place every year here. Every year they put the press off into the corner. They act as if they don't want their pictures taken and get good publicity so they can saturate their sinister, political dealings, you know what I mean."

"Yes," Patrick said, following alongside Mr. Law as they walked through the very crowded concourse of the Commons Center. This was the perfect place to do the assassination. It was dimly lit and well populated. It had the down points like the surveillance cameras everywhere, but that did not matter. Thousands of faces could be lost easily among each other; a bullet comes from a cell phone and no one would ever know who pulled the trigger. The only thing they might get was the direction from which the bullets came from. Patrick had special padding in his shoes for the running that would be involved for tonight's getaway. If they did not catch him tonight, they never would, Patrick was sure. Mr. Law continued to babble on.

"I mean, the press makes these old blokes nowadays. When it comes to elections and things of the sort, they try to reach out to people as much as humanly bloody possible so that people can hear what their 'plans' are all about so they can get votes or what not."

"Yeah," Patrick said as if he was following the conversation.

"I mean, they need us, if you know what I mean. In this day and age, the elections are based on what the press runs. These people, and you and I, we don't vote for who we actually want. We vote for who the press tells us to vote for. We pick up magazines and go on the Internet and read what other people say and tell ourselves 'that's horrible what these blokes are doing,' or maybe, 'that's what great Mr. or Ms. So-And-So is doing.' You know what I mean, mate?"

"Yeah," Patrick said trying to speed up in their decreasing walking pace. Patrick needed to find out where the press room was so he could abandon this man who was talking about nothing.

The guy just couldn't stop talking. He continued, "Some prints or television shows will portray a certain person as a savior, and the other magazine or paper will portray that same man as a horrible choice to be a leader. All depends on what you read, if you know what I mean, mate. We make these lying blokes who they are. You know what I mean?

"Yeah," Patrick responded trying to be as short with this British gentleman as possible. "I know what you mean."

"What press company did you say you were from again, mate?"

Patrick had forgotten what he told the man earlier and what was on his home-made badge. Other things were on his mind. He recollected for a moment, pausing. "A Canadian Internet news website. Look here," Patrick said as he turned his badge around to face the front and presented it before Mr. Law in a sideways position so he could read it, also. "Inside Out Canada Online."

"Ah, yes. How is it working for an online periodical?"

"It's nice. Flexible hours."

"Really?" They had arrived to the press area. Patrick told the annoying friendly Mr. Law that he needed to use the facilities and that he would be back to talk to him about politics and so on when he returned—he wasn't. He knew where the press area was now, and he would do his best upon returning to avoid the Mr. Law.

He walked over toward the sign that read "Toilette." He walked in busily to avoid any other friendly reporters that wanted to socialize. After flushing the urinal, he noticed that the water in the toilet swirled clockwise. Odd, he thought. He proceeded to wash his hands, and then exited the *toilette*.

* * *

The Commons Convention Center was set up like a very small coliseum. There were tables all along the concourse that aligned the square-shaped main floor. Down on the main floor, all of the rich and famous ate. In a separate corridor in the coliseum, surrounded by security, was the Premier Zurich Dining Hall where the world leaders ate for this special annual occasion.

Gordon and Pamela were seated at the huge round table at the five o'clock point from the grand entrance door in the Dining Hall. Even though all the world leaders were seated around the table with each other, there was a separate waiter for each couple. An English waitress waited on the UK Prime Minister and his wife, A French waiter for the French president and his wife, and so forth.

Everything was going smoothly. After everyone had eaten dinner and ordered desert, Gordon would commence to give the signal for the Baricon to move in. The plan was perfectly arranged.

Gordon would announce a special surprise and invite a few guests into the Dining Hall who were waiting right outside. The guests would put a gun to Gordon's head which he would actually get from Gordon's waist (because Gordon did not have to go through a security check when arriving, seeing as he was president and all). Then, the remainder of the team would move in, a few Secret Service agents and other body guards from the other countries would get knocked off, and the Baricon leaders would take all the wives away. Then Gordon would start making his demands.

He had the whole kit with international treaty contracts (which were just for show) and the laptop in which he would enter the nuclear access codes in to obtain the power to use the warheads—it was actually as simply as that, in theory. And he figured he could do this, he was, after all, not only the President of the United States but the Constitutional Dictator of the United States. He already had control of a quarter of the nuclear weapons on the planet. If all did not go as planned with the access codes, Gordon had it all worked out so that a single phone call would blow up a city or two in the unlikely case that a country did not comply. He would be fully in control of everything...in theory.

Patrick was here to make sure the president's plan did not work out precisely, or at all, like Gordon wanted it to.

Gordon smiled at his wife. "What would you like to eat, dear?"

"I think I'll go with a little chicken parmesan and a glass French Cabernet for tonight."

"I think I will have the same," Gordon told the waitress. They did their camera smiles as the media walked in to take pictures of the round table of world leader. "Did I ever tell you what a beautiful smile you have?" Gordon said just to be saying something.

His mind was in a million different places and he did not want it to be apparent.

"Thank you, dear. To tell you the truth though, I can't wait to get out of here."

"I thought you wanted to come."

"I did, my love. However, your amazingly handsome face prompts me to desire for the occurrences of later on in the evening."

Gordon gulped. "I can't wait either," he said trying to sound like there was actually going to be a *later in the evening* for them. There would be a later in the evening, but he did not think it would be quite what she had in mind. All of a sudden he saw a face that looked amazingly familiar. Where had he seen this face? He widened his eyes in dread, as he unknowingly looked down the barrel of Patrick's cell phone.

"What's the matter, dear?" Pamela asked Gordon, looking at her husband, concerned. "Dear?" she chimed trying to catch his attention. She looked over to where he was staring. As Gordon hopelessly jumped to his feet as quickly as he possibly could, two shots were fired from Patrick's cell phone.

CHAPTER XVIII

He wasn't dead, he realized. He never thought he would be shot. It seemed like everything happened at once. People started screaming and Gordon just fell back. A Secret Service agent caught him before he could hit the ground. It was loud but very quiet at the same time from his present sonic perception. Once the bullet hit his chest, he heard his own heart beating, sounding as if it was straining desperately, trying to keep blood pumping. He heard a beat, then nothing. *Beat,* he prayed—just keeping beating. It beat again.

The screams of everyone filled his ears yet the noise of it all did not seem to make it past his ears into his head. It was peaceful for him even as chaos was unleashed all around him. He was covered my Secret Service agents who kept yelling, "Get the meds! Get the meds! Call for help! The president's down!"

He was down. *Who shot me,* he asked himself. *Who was it? Who wanted me dead? Where'd the bullet come from? Who got a gun beyond security? Hadn't the entire perimeter been secured days before I arrived? Who could possibly pull this off? Is this my end? Who shot me?*

Gordon was suddenly being rushed somewhere; he didn't know where; he was just along for the miserable ride. "Move! Move! Out of the way! Get out of the way! Move! Move! Get out of the way!" he heard as his body was carried across a room full of yelling women and, for this special episode, shrieking men. Grown men were screaming, yelling, and running around franticly. These were the valiant, brave leaders of superpower countries, yelling like little school girls.

"Out of the way! Move! Move!" he kept hearing as he was carried though the frantic crowd. *Where had the bullet hit*, he wondered. *Lord, don't let it have hit a vital organ! It couldn't have hit a vital organ. I would be dead by now*, he reassured himself. *It just wouldn't be right for me to die here, now. It can't be! I can't die*, he yelled in his head as his life went back and forth, as he faded from life to death, from death to life. And he was conscious during the entire ride.

* * *

The truth of the matter is (even for the President of the United States) death has absolutely no consideration for people's feelings. It has no regard for who a person is, what a person has done in life, or what that person would have been. The reality is that death is impartial, like nature, to all circumstances outside of itself. Once a person's number has been pulled, it's over. There are no pardons.

Some straddle the fence, going from life to death like Gordon was experiencing after he was shot. Some make it; some don't. Death can come without warning, without a sign, without a notice so that a person does not have the opportunity to set their affairs in order. No human can negotiate with death and convince it to diverge from the law of nature.

Sometimes it's sudden; sometimes it occurs over a period of time—the transition from being alive to dead. Sometimes it is painful; sometimes there is no pain at all. And even sometimes, there is a feeling of jubilation associated with it. Gordon felt the pain, but it was not from the bullet's impact on him. He was suffering from the thought of his wife. He was dying with a lie, and it hurt.

Nothing in the world can hurt more than dying without the chance to tell that most dearly loved one the truth. Nothing can hurt worse than not having the chance to set things right which a person set so wrong in life. Gordon was going through the worst. And, he was dying of it.

* * *

I'm passing away from all this, he realized. "Where is she," he asked himself actually getting this out of his mouth. "Where...is she?" he asked in a bewildered, mumbling voice.

"*Shhh*, Mr. President. Save your energy. We're getting you help. Just hold on. Save your energy," someone told him.

"Where...is...she?"

"Please—save your energy. It will be okay. Lay him here! The meds are here!"

"Where is...she?" he got out again.

"*Shhh*," he heard again. At that moment, the meds were hovering over the wounded president. His shirt was quickly unbuttoned and opened so that his chest lay exposed and accessible to the only humans who could save him now. His chest became more colorful with red as more and more blood left his body. He was gasping, and they were moving quicker with every second's pass.

"Compression patches!" one of them yelled. Swiftly, upon the request for the compression patches, swabs of the patches were being pressed on the gasping president's chest. The compression patches that the emergency team was using were to stop the copious amount of blood that was emerging from Gordon's chest.

The heart monitor was then hooked up to him. Blood was wiped, and the heart monitor electrodes were attached. They put an electrode on his upper chest near his heart and one on his stomach to have two indicators of his heart rate. His heart rate was not that stupendous, going at the rate of a little under fifty beats per minute. "We may be able to keep him, if we get him to a hospital quickly!" he heard someone exclaim.

Short on breaths, heartbeats, but not pain, he laid there with his eyes half open as people were rushing around him, trying to save him. He felt an abrupt electrical shock run through his chest. His heart began to beat faster. He was provided hope—his heart was getting a boost. His heart rate moved up abruptly, and then gradually escaladed to an almost normal heart rate.

Lord, let me cheat death, he prayed. *Just give me this chance. Just give me a chance to set it all right.* He prayed and begged as if he had been nothing less than saint all his life and deserved to live.

Either air was getting shorter or his lungs were deflating at a fatal tempo, he realized, gasping for air, gasping for survival. He spoke swiftly with incoherent mumbles, "I can't breathe. I can't breathe. I need air. I can't breathe."

"Shhhh. Save your energy," he kept hearing, along with the constant confusion of people saying, "Move! Get out of the way! Move! Get the stretcher! Is he stable?! His he alive?! Put him down! Pick him up! Move!"

He decided to save his energy after all, because they could not hear him. His life was in their (hopefully) very skilled hands. *Save me*, he prayed. *Protect my wife. Don't let anything happen to my wife*, he begged upon deaf ears (or rather, from a vocally-challenged mouth).

It had been only fifteen seconds since he had been shot when a stretcher arrived, running over his right hand. His brain could not translate the pain from his hand, because it was so preoccupied with so many other painful signals from his self-afflicting thoughts and that hurt worse than the bullet wounds. Sprawled out on the floor, chest out, bloody, patched, covered by emergency meds, and dying, he was lifted up onto the stretcher that had so gracefully crushed probably numerous bones in his knuckles. The heart monitor that was equipped with an automatic electric defibrillator, which sent electricity soaring through his body when his heart rate declined, was lifted up with him onto the emergency stretcher.

Gordon had heard it all, but it was remarkably peaceful, serene, quiet. This had to be death, or just a really bad trick. *There is no white light*, he reasoned with himself as he laid on the stretcher motionless.

He heard the patter of hastily moving feet. He heard the frantic voices around him yelling, "Move him quick! Run! Be careful! That way!" He heard this along with other yells and cries and curses. "No pictures! Get back!" he heard. Everything seemed to get louder and louder as the tension seemed to rise higher and higher. Yet, at the same time, he heard nothing. The volume in the room seemed to decline as everything appeared as if it were fading more and more. It had faded—his eyes closed completely, and he saw...but darkness.

The electrodes from the monitor quickly noted how Gordon's heart was halting in beats and quickly shocked him. Nothing. They shocked again. His heart rate began to slowly increase. It dropped for a moment, everyone held their breaths, and then it rose gradually. Emotions were going back and forth with hope and fear as Gordon's heart ventured from motion to immobility.

In a but very short period of riding in the ambulance, he was being rushed into the emergency room of the University of Zurich Hospital. *"Eine Kugel in seiner Brust. Er ist in kritischem Zustand,"* the one of the emergency meds said to the nurses in the emergency room. German for: This man has a bullet shot to the chest. He's in critical condition.

"Get him a doctor! We need a doctor!" one of the Servicemen demanded.

"We need a doctor! Who speaks good English?!" the Servicemen collectively demanded to know. There were no responses as Gordon was lying on the stretcher being transported down a hall.

Gordon found himself lying on the table, still motionless. The Servicemen occupying the entire room. The nurses were asking them nicely in Swiss, German, and even English to leave the room, but none of them complied with the hospital staff's orders. The seven agents in the room stayed, watching. Two agents secured the door, watching out for any more attempts on the president's life. They knew the chances were slim to none, but it was their job always to protect the president. They had surely failed in that regard on this day.

Gordon was constantly being shocked by the electrodes that were attached to him, as his heartbeat kept failing. He was unresponsive, and his eyes were closed, but he was there—he could hear everything. Though, his mind was not in the room. His mind might as well not even have been attached to his body as he laid in the emergency room thinking of only one thing. He could only think of her. *Was she okay*, he wondered as he felt his heartbeat pause. His heart seemed to have this reoccurring theme of not being able to sustain itself.

He was hooked up to every possible machine they could think to hook him up to. The blood that was still running from his chest was being pressed down with more swabs of compression patches.

* * *

Meanwhile, Pamela had been rushed to another location. This location: to the safest location in Switzerland. Once Gordon was shot and the meds had arrived, an order had been made to have her moved to an undisclosed locality. This locality was so undisclosed that she wasn't even privy as to where they were taking her. She was seated in one of the Cruisers that was expeditiously traveling out of Zurich. She was in the car for about thirty minutes before they reached what appeared a military base.

"Is he alive?!" she insisted to know for the millionth time. "Where is my husband?" She was in tears, her Mascara smeared over her face. Many handkerchiefs were presented before her. She demanded that they get the handkerchiefs out of her face along with screaming other verbal indecencies.

"Your husband is being helped in one of the Zurich hospitals now, Mrs. First Lady. We are taking you somewhere safe."

The Service agent's phone rang. He nodded and said, "Good." He hung up and looked at Pamela. "They got the man that shot your husband. He was taken down outside the Commons Center. He's dead now."

"I don't give a damn about him! My husband shouldn't have been shot in the first place! That was your job to ensure that! You shot my husband! You shot him!"

"Mrs. Wade..."

"Take me to my husband! I want to see him! You listen to me! I don't care what your orders are! That doesn't mean a *goddamn* thing right now! You take me to my husband or I will get out of this car and go to him myself!" she exclaimed in a tone that could make the Devil himself quiver in fear and meet her every request.

"I'm sorry, Mrs. First Lady. That is highly impossible right now. We must look after your safety for the present. I'm sorry."

"I don't want to hear that you're sorry! I want to here you say we are going to the hospital where my husband is. You tell me that right now!"

"Mrs. Wade, I understand you're concern. I'm just as concerned as you are."

"Stop!" she commanded, transitioning to a lower tone. "You stop that now. You have...*no* idea how concerned I am." The Servicemen swallowed his words very quickly. "You have no idea. Don't say you do. You have none! Not an inkling, not a bit, not even a crumb of concern as much as I feel right now. You find a way to get me to that hospital and take me there right now. Or, I swear..." This lady was very serious, the agent established quite quickly after she basically slapped him in the face with her potently words. It also seemed as if she would actually do something physically in a bit—the way this was going.

"I apologize. Sincerely, Mrs. Wade. What I said was out of line. I have no idea. And I promise, Mrs. Wade, I will get you to him as soon as possible. I would take you to the hospital immediately, but I simply can't. I have to follow orders. It is not my decision. I'm not the one who is making the call."

"Then, let me talk to person making the call." The Cruiser had stopped, and her door was opened.

"Mrs. Wade," the agent who opened the door beckoned. She ignored him, still looking at the agent in the car.

"Who is making the call?" she asked.

"Mrs. President," the agent standing outside the car summoned again.

She looked at the agent outside the car with the hardest look ever given by a human being. "Shut the hell up." And it was so. He shut the hell up. She looked back at the agent in the car. "Who made the call?" she asked again. "You tell me. I'm not going to ask you again. Who made the call?"

"It's not in my hands?"

"Who made the *goddamn* call?"

"It's protocol, Mrs. Wade. We have to protect you."

"I don't want to hear that! You were supposed to do that for my husband!" And what could the agent say to that? Nothing. He couldn't say anything. "Look," she continued, fierce with eyes full of fire, "I don't care about 'protocol.' You take me to my husband." There was a moment of silence as she stared the poor agent down to the size of an ant.

"Close the door," he told the agent standing outside the car. "We're going to the hospital." He looked back at her. "Are you happy now?"

She looked at him hard and uttered not a word. With her eyes, she shrunk him even smaller. The car was restarted and they made a U-turn, leaving the base. Destination: University of Zurich Hospital.

They arrived, and surrounded by even more Secret Service than she arrived with, Pamela swiftly made her way up the stairs outside the hospital. She walked into the emergency room where several security guards tried to stop her and her entourage of agents from entering into the emergency section—the hospital security guards were politely moved out of the way by the US Secret Service.

She wept. She heard so much panic. The nurses were telling

the agents to stay clear of the area, and the agents didn't comply once again. Pamela took off toward her husband.

"Is he okay? Let me see him!"

"I'm sorry, Mrs. Wade. The doctor has requested that there be no visitors in this room. They are working on him right now," sternly informed one of the agents at the door.

"Will he be okay?"

"We hope so. We truly hope so. We don't know much now, however. The doctor came in about an hour ago and began helping him."

"Is he in critical condition?"

"I can't guess what condition he's in. Everyone is speaking Swiss and German. We have a few agents who speak proficient Swiss and German, and we've been able to understand that he does have a chance of survival. However, he seems to be shifting in and out, and they don't know for sure what's going to happen. All we can do is pray."

"Is he conscious? Is he breathing okay? Is he on life support? What are they doing?"

"As far as him being conscious, I saw him mumbling a few things that I couldn't understand at the Commons Center. He's just been in an out it seems, from the times that I saw him. I believe he'll pull through, Mrs. First Lady."

"Is that what the meds said?"

"No, Mrs. Wade, but I have faith, and I believe. I know this can be a tough thing to go through, but you have to stay prayerful. That's the best route to go in this situation. He'll pull though."

"Thank you," she said with a bit of relief. She was somewhat calmer as she walked over to the chair across the room and sat on the wooden bench. As she sat on the bench, she bowed her head. She wept more.

"Lord, my husband *needs* you now. Lord, save my dear husband. He means the world to me. Lord, show yourself today and lift Gordon from the pain, from the suffering that he is enduring. Bless his organs, any of them that were affected by the gunshots. I rebuke any demons from taking the life of my husband in Your name O Father Almighty. Keep my husband. I claim victory right now for the life of my husband. I claim life, by God. Please Lord, don't let him pass. He's a great leader of men, and even a greater husband. Don't tell him die. Don't let my husband die. Please O Lord! I won't be able to live without him here. Please, save him."

Behind the closed doors of the room in front of her, Gordon's heart rate dropped dramatically. The electrodes shocked him for the seventh time of the night to keep his heart beating. It did no good this time. "Oh my God, are we losing him?" asked one of the agents to the doctor who was yelling off some crazy German at all the nurses, her words streaming together in very rapid succession. *God, save him!*

The heart monitor which was making a constant repetitious series of beeps, now was sounding off a flat-line beep which had the effect of making everyone in the room panic even more in an unnerved manner. The doctor was unleashing more Swiss or German, or maybe both, very speedily as the clock ran down. They pulled out a larger defibrillator, yelled something in Swiss, and shocked away, hoping to get his heart beating once again. In turn, his heart started beating once more (probably out of fear of another powerful shock).

Five minutes had passed at a normal heart rate, and he was regaining consciousness. The first thing he asked was, "Where's my wife?"

"She's outside the door in the hall. They don't feel you should have any visitors at this time. Do you feel okay?"

"I need to see my wife."

"But Mr. President—"

"That's an order."

"But—"

"Bring me my wife."

Upon Gordon's order, his wife walked in. "Gordon," she said as she placed her left hand gently under his chin, her right hand on the top of his head. "Oh, Gordon! Are you alright?"

"I'm sorry."

"It's okay, dear. *Shh*, don't say anything. They say you'll be fine. You're going to pull through, okay."

"My journal. In our room. In my dresser."

"*Shh.*"

"Listen to me."

"I'm listening."

"Read it." Then, he passed away; a flat-line sounded once again—this time, indefinitely.

* * *

Until the moment Gordon met death he didn't realize that it was Lannigan all this time. His old buddy, his running mate, his successor, his traitor. *Lannigan had my assassination planned all along.*

CHAPTER XIX

Fourteen hours later, Pamela was in their bedroom in the White House reading the last page of Gordon's journal.

* * *

Pamela, if you are reading this, I must be dead. In this journal are half page accounts of my life in the White House. The missing halves of each page were torn and burned 24 hours after each entry was completed. It is my final wish that you destroy this journal after reading the entirety of what is contained. My reason for leaving half sheets in this journal can be simply explained. Throughout our relationship, I only told you half-truths. These, in turn, are the second halves.

I led a private life of lies and deceit for many years. I am, what you could call a terrorist, a traitor to my country, and a good ol' Quisling of Norway or Petain of France. Moreover, it seems that I have received a similar fate as these two notorious traitors.

I have secretly been a member of the Baricon organization since college. Remember my good friend Muhammad Nahas? In my junior year of undergrad, I pledged my secret allegiance to the Baricon under the sponsorship of Nahas' family.

Did I want to betray the country that I was born and raised in? I truly hope that you would never believe that. Did I enjoy lying to you? I hope you would never believe that I did. I'm not sure what consolation this will provide, but falling in love with you was a blunder and never part of my intention while we dated before marriage. However, as fate would hold it, I fell deliriously in love with you. I sincerely hope that you believe this. I love you, and have loved you, with all my heart, since the first day I met you.

I could imagine that you would ask why. Why was I ever associated with a band of Middle Eastern extremists? The sake of humanity is my sole answer, as odd as it may seem. During the Cold War in the 60s and 70s, the United States possessed thousands of nuclear weapons; also, the unstable Soviet Union and China had almost equivalent nuclear threats. Together, we three countries were fatal threats to the world. Throughout the history of nuclear arms, leaders around the world have tried to resolve issues in ways that could have driven us into nuclear winter. It was theorized that the only possible resolve to the nuclear threat of annihilation of the entire human race was simply the annihilation of nuclear arms.

It is truly a miracle that a great majority of the world's population has not yet been obliterated. Grave mistakes were made during the Cold War and these sad years that followed; as a consequence, major problems arose. The world was in need of a solution. The Baricon found a solution. I pledged to that solution. I believed in the solution to fight evil with evil, death with death. As a result, it appears as though I died for that solution.

I'm sorry, Pam. You are the world to me. I questioned myself so many times, and so many times I wanted to tell you. And what does that say about me? We both know that it's not your intentions or what you say in life that defines you, but rather what you do. I have failed a country, I have failed a world, but before I did all of that, I failed you. I'm responsible for the deaths of thousands of my own people, myself, and us. My culpability could hold up in ranks with the atrocious acts of Hitler; I am no better of a man.

The truth of the matter is, dear, I never deserved you. You are my world; I should have spared you from this. I know that my deepest apologies mean nothing to you nor the number of times I could apologize for this. The truth is, dear, you can't fight evil with evil. I learned this lesson too late.

I only have one request of you in my death: Please don't turn the cold shoulder on me. I still live through these memoirs and letters—please, destroy all of me. Don't allow the world to know what I did. Let me die.

* * *

His journal falls from her hands to the floor. Her shaking hands grip her heated face as tears pour through the cracks between her fingers. She loses her breath as air lunges in and out of her at an abnormally fast rate. She lets out a high-pitched scream as she falls sideways from her husband's favorite chair onto the floor. Again, she screams. The sound-proof walls prevent anyone from hearing her cry. Lying there, she painfully suffers in her own anguish. She feels the pain in her chest as she endures the heartache from the overwhelming revelations revealed from the pages of her late husband's journal.

"Lies!" she cries. "All lies!" Chills run rapidly up and down her back and spread throughout her body. She bangs the wooden floor with her right fist. Tear drops hit the floor as she bangs harder and harder until her arm finally gives out and her entire body collapses. Face down on the floor, she moans agonizingly, *"Why!?"* as her voice breaks and nothing but wheezes escape from her mouth. Her head becomes hotter, and her cheeks become tense. She rolls over slowly onto her back as more tears roll down her face without direction; she feels some run into her ears; she tastes others as they run into her mouth. The questions of *why* haunt her in her heated, impassioned mourning. She desperately tries to answer the questions that bombard her mind all at once. *Did he truly love me? Why would he lie to me? What else had he lied about? Why me?*

She lets out an intense, deafening scream that temporarily impairs her own ears. But what do her ears matter? *What matters?* Screaming more, she picks up the journal that fell with her and throws it with a vengeance at the mirror that stands across the room. It bounces off the mirror, falling once again to the floor. Quickly, she rises and runs towards the mirror. Upon seeing her reflection, she strikes the mirror with her fist, penetrating it with her wedding ring, causing the mirror to shatter. Pieces of the mirror dart onto the floor and some into her flesh. But what do either of these matter, floor or flesh? She falls onto the glass, painfully absorbing the sharp incisions as her blood stains some of the scattered pieces. She looks down at one of the bigger pieces of mirror. It is sharp and fairly resembles a dagger. She lets out another cry as she looks into her eyes through the dagger-shaped piece.

Sitting up, she grasps the dagger with both hands and raises it from the floor up towards her face. She extends her arms so that they are straight, the point of the dagger pointing towards the floor. She grips it tightly, releases the sharp piece of mirror with her blood-drenched right hand to wipe the tears from her eyes, and regains her grasp even tighter. With great force, she impels it into her stomach. She gasps for breath and falls to the floor. Before she can die from her own self-affliction, her heartache kills her first. Her eyes close as she lies dead, her husband's journal laying next to her.

* * *

Hours later, Lannigan walks into their bedroom. He smiles. He orders that the journal be burned to ashes.

* * *

This was the story of the president, his wife, and the events that history would not mention.

Acknowledgments

Witness an example that the Lord is able,
Eternally,
I depend on Christ, the holiest and most stable,
I write fiction, but His words are no fable.

Thank you, mom, dad, Mariah, and Ben.
Thanks to all those who contributed towards the technical aspects of my book. Emily Fifer, my editor and friend. Bertha Crawford, a wonderful critic. Detective Butterick and Sergeant Mills, mentors during my internship at the investigation bureau. Racheal and Rhonda Howard, great supporters. Mr. Sanders and Dr. Watson, my mock trial coaches.

Special thanks to all of the teachers who reprimanded me for seeking original thought. I appreciate the motivation.

This novel is dedicated to the memory of my grandmother and Okechi Womeodu.

Meet the Author

Michael De'Shazer II is a seventeen year-old senior in high school in Memphis, TN. This is his first novel.

To learn more about the author and *The Wade Scandal*, visit www.wadescandal.com